ACCLAIM FOR

THE ROYAL

"This is classic romance at its very best."

—DEBBIE MACOMBER, #1 *NEW YORK TIMES* BESTSELLING AUTHOR

"Perfect for Valentine's Day, Hauck's latest inspirational romance offers an uplifting and emotionally rewarding tale that will delight her growing fan base."

—*LIBRARY JOURNAL*, STARRED REVIEW

"Hauck writes a feel-good novel that explores the trauma and love of the human heart . . . an example of patience and sacrifice that readers will adore."

—*ROMANTIC TIMES*, 4 STARS

"A stirring modern-day fairy tale about the power of true love."

—CINDY KIRK, AUTHOR OF *LOVE AT MISTLETOE INN*

"*How to Catch a Prince* is an enchanting story told with bold flavor and tender insight. Engaging characters come alive as romance blooms between a prince and his one true love. Hauck's own brand of royal-style romance shines in this third installment of the Royal Wedding series."

—DENISE HUNTER, BESTSELLING AUTHOR OF *BOOKSHOP BY THE SEA*

"*How to Catch a Prince* contains all the elements I've come to love in Rachel Hauck's Royal Wedding series: an 'it don't come easy' happily ever after, a contemporary romance woven through with royal history, and a strong spiritual thread with an unexpected touch of the divine. Hauck's smooth writing—and the way she wove life truths throughout the novel—made for a couldn't-put-it-down read."

—BETH K. VOGT, AUTHOR OF *SOMEBODY LIKE YOU*,
ONE OF *PUBLISHERS WEEKLY*'S BEST BOOKS OF 2014

"Rachel Hauck's inspiring Royal Wedding series is one for which you should reserve space on your keeper shelf!"

—*USA Today*

"Hauck spins a surprisingly believable royal-meets-commoner love story. This is a modern and engaging tale with well-developed secondary characters that are entertaining and add a quirky touch. Hauck fans will find a gem of a tale."

—*Publishers Weekly* starred review of *Once Upon a Prince*

The Wedding Shop

"I adored *The Wedding Shop*! Rachel Hauck has created a tender, nostalgic story, weaving together two pairs of star-crossed lovers from the present and the past with the magical space that connects them. So full of heart and heartache and redemption, this book is one you'll read long into the night, until the characters become your friends, and Heart's Bend, Tennessee, your second hometown."

—Beatriz Williams, *New York Times* bestselling author

"*The Wedding Shop* is the kind of book I love, complete with flawed yet realistic characters, dual timelines that intersect unexpectedly, a touch of magic, and a large dose of faith. Two breathtaking romances are the perfect bookends for this novel about love, forgiveness, and following your dreams. And a stunning, antique wedding dress with a secret of its own. This is more than just a good read—it's a book to savor."

—Karen White, *New York Times* bestselling author

The Wedding Chapel

"Hauck's engaging novel about love, forgiveness, and new beginnings adeptly ties together multiple oscillating storylines of several generations of families. Interesting plot interweaves romance, real life issues, and a dash of mystery . . . Recommend for mature fans of well-done historical fiction. "

—*CBA RETAILERS AND RESOURCES*

"Hauck tells another gorgeously rendered story. The raw, hidden emotions of Taylor and Jack are incredibly realistic and will resonate with readers. The way the entire tale comes together with the image of the chapel as holding the heartbeat of God is breathtaking and complements the romance of the story."

—*ROMANTIC TIMES*, 4 ^{1}/2 STARS AND A TOP PICK!

THE WEDDING DRESS

"*The Wedding Dress* is a thought-provoking read and one of the best books I have read. Look forward to more . . ."

—MICHELLE JOHNMAN, GOLD COAST, AUSTRALIA

"I thank God for your talent and that you wrote *The Wedding Dress*. I will definitely come back to this book and read it again. And now I cannot wait to read *Once Upon a Prince*."

—AGATA FROM POLAND

A Royal Christmas Wedding

Also by Rachel Hauck

The Fifth Avenue Story Society
The Memory House
The Love Letter
The Writing Desk
The Wedding Dress
The Wedding Chapel
The Wedding Shop
The Wedding Dress Christmas

Novellas found in A Year of Weddings

A March Bride included in *Spring Brides*
A Brush with Love: A January Wedding Story included in *Say I Do*

The Royal Wedding Series

Once Upon a Prince
Princess Ever After
How to Catch a Prince
A Royal Christmas Wedding

Lowcountry Romance Novels

Sweet Caroline
Love Starts with Elle
Dining with Joy

Nashville Novels

Nashville Dreams
Nashville Sweetheart

With Sara Evans

Sweet By and By
Softly and Tenderly
Love Lifted Me

A Royal Christmas Wedding

THE ROYAL WEDDING SERIES

RACHEL HAUCK

THOMAS NELSON
Since 1798

Published in Nashville, Tennessee, by Thomas Nelson. Thomas Nelson is a registered trademark of HarperCollins Christian Publishing, Inc.

Thomas Nelson titles may be purchased in bulk for educational, business, fundraising, or sales promotional use. For information, please e-mail SpecialMarkets@ ThomasNelson.com.

Publisher's Note: This novel is a work of fiction. Names, characters, places, and incidents are either products of the author's imagination or used fictitiously. All characters are fictional, and any similarity to people living or dead is purely coincidental.

ISBN 978-0-310-34481-0 (ebook)
ISBN 978-0-310-35045-3 (audio download)
ISBN 978-0-7852-3322-0 (mass market)
ISBN 978-0-7852-6281-7 (repack)

Library of Congress Cataloging-in-Publication Data

Names: Hauck, Rachel, 1960-, author.
Title: A royal Christmas wedding / Rachel Hauck.
Description: Grand Rapids, Michigan: Zondervan, [2016] | Series: Royal wedding series; 4
Identifiers: LCCN 2016018246 | ISBN 9780310344537 (paperback)
Subjects: | GSAFD: Christian fiction. | Love stories.
Classification: LCC PS3608.A866 R69 2016 | DDC 813/.6—dc23 LC record available at https://lccn.loc.gov/2016018246

Printed in the United States of America

21 22 23 24 25 / LSC / 5 4 3 2 1

To all those who dare to dream

PROLOGUE

Brighton Kingdom
1834

The night was moonless, the color of black ink, with not one star twinkling from the heavens. The air, cold and brisk, swirled with snow.

The ancients called such darkness the Boot of God. But for Prince Michael there was no darkness. The glow of gaslights along the palace grounds and the love beaming in his heart showed him the way.

Lady Charlene offered a challenge. And he intended to take it.

Running along the perimeter, past the reach of the lights, Michael aimed for Pembroke Chapel and its notorious bell tower.

"Mick, ole chap, what's lit your fire?" The voice of his mate Paulson slipped over his shoulder. "The music, the food, pints of bitters, and all the pretty ladies are back in the ballroom, the latter just waiting for us to dance."

"Don't slow me, Pauls. I'm going to ring the chapel bell." Michael worked the heavy iron latch of the tower's door until it sprang open.

"What? You jest. And what unsuspecting damsel will be the object of your unwanted affection?" Paulson's steps neared, his breathing heavy, his lantern adding light.

"If I tell you, what will be the mystery?" Michael started up the slick stone steps of Pembroke Chapel bell tower in the dark, feeling his way and balancing with his hand on the rickety wood railing.

Tonight he wanted nothing more than to ring the chapel bell at midnight—according to the Harvest Celebration tradition— declaring his love for Lady Charlene and his intention to marry her on Christmas Day.

One hundred and eighty-two narrow steps and he'd arrive at the top of the tower.

Paulson's voice echoed from below. "If you ring that bell, everyone will want to know who your intended is. You won't escape, ole man. What of your father? He'll have a word or two to say."

"He'll discover the truth on Christmas morn. Like everyone else. Who am I to break with a good Brighton tradition by revealing the woman of my affection?"

At the top, Michael butted against the copula, forcing the rusty hinges to give way until he stood under the four-hundred-year-old bell.

Paulson arrived a moment later, the lantern swinging from his hand, the golden light reflecting in his wide smile. "There's your bell. What seems to be the delay, my good man?" He motioned to the bell cord. "Or did you knock some sense into yourself banging against the door?"

"The cord . . ." Michael yanked on the twisted hemp rope attached to a hook in the tower stone. "It won't budge. It's frozen."

"Thank the heavens, you're saved."

"I don't want to be saved." Michael, determined, rubbed his hands together, gripped the rope, and leaned, his muscles taut under his winter coat.

"Mick, stop, think. What will you do after you ring the bell and realize you must marry the woman of your ardor? Brighton traditions are almost as sacred as Holy Scripture, I do believe. You can't change your mind, citing cowardice and whatnot."

"My feet are plenty warm, thank you. I will marry her. Christmas morning at Watchman Abbey. As tradition bids me. There'll be no breach of sanctity on my part. Now, make yourself useful. Give me a hand."

With Paulson's help, Michael freed the cord from its hook just as the glorious cathedral bells chimed throughout Brighton's capital, Cathedral City.

When the last chime sounded, marking the dawn of a new day, the end of the harvest, and the beginning of Christmas season, Michael would ring the chapel bell, the lone sound indicating to all that there would be a royal wedding on Christmas Day.

If, however, brave prince won fair maiden's heart.

"You've gone daft, man." Paulson stamped his foot, the sound echoing through the stiff air. "How many poor sods, all of them princes and noblemen, I might add, have run these chapel steps? Declaring their true love only to end up at Watchman Abbey alone with no bride and, I dare say, no pride as the hounds of the press nipped at their heels?"

Michael leaned against the wall, the cold rope in his sweating hands, counting the cathedral chimes.

3

Four . . . five . . .

"My fate is not another man's, Pauls."

"Something's afoot. Out with it." Setting the lantern on the base of the open archway facing the city, Paulson grabbed the cord. "For whom doth this bell toll?"

"Charlene." Michael met his friend's gaze in the flickering lantern light. "But now you are sworn to secrecy. Not a word of it."

Paulson stepped into Michael, wrenching the damp, worn hemp rope from his hands. "Lady Charlene of Clounnaught?" His expression, his tone, his posture mirrored that of the chapel construction—cold, hard as stone. "Are you trying to vex me?"

The air vibrated with the resonating sound of the city's cathedral bells.

Six . . . seven . . .

"Vex you? What on earth, man?" Michael took hold of the rope, using his might to twist it from Paulson's hands. But to no avail.

"Charlene and I are to be pledged. You know this with certainty."

"I know no such thing. If your words are true, why has her father not made the announcement? Why are you not already pledged? You're both of age."

"When the hour is right. I've commercial investments yet to be settled as well as my position with Father's barrister house. But if you ring this bell, good man, with intentions for Lady Charlene, we will be at war, you and I."

"Let the battle begin." Michael slammed into Paulson, freeing the cord from his hands as the city bells peeled through him, through the tower, and through the cold.

Eight . . . nine . . . ten . . .

Paulson, the son of the Earl of Granite, raised his hand against Michael's throat. "I will defeat you, Michael. Try me not."

Unable to breathe, Michael desperately stomped on Paulson's foot. With a yelp, he released the prince.

"Try *me* not. She all but told me should I ring the bell, she will marry me."

"Ha! How is that keeping with tradition? Nevertheless, her father will have the last word."

Eleven . . . twelve.

The bells tolled one last time from the great cathedrals in the city, the tone vibrating across the palace grounds.

"A prince against an earl? I believe she's all but mine." Michael shoved his hand into Paulson's chest. "Stand aside while I ring the bell."

Gripping high on the thick rope, he pulled, leaning, putting the six-hundred-pound bell into motion. "For Lady Charlene, for Lady Charlene."

Paulson peered through the arches. "The palace doors are opening. I can see the glow from the ballroom."

Michael focused on ringing the bell up, tugging on the rope, letting it slip through his hands, then pulling again, the rope releasing higher and higher.

The singular chime rang higher and louder.

"People are exiting the ballroom." Paulson snatched up his light and made for the stairs. "Lanterns are bobbing all over the grounds. They're coming this way, bloke."

At last, the bell was in full motion. Michael released the rope and followed the light of the swaying lantern.

"Out of my way, Paulson. I must be the first down."

"Well then, I consider that a challenge." Paulson turned, shoved

Michael so he crashed against the stone wall, his feet slipping down the steps. He clamored to reach the railing and steady himself.

"Paulson, stop." Michael gained his balance and felt his way down the treacherous stairwell, the light of the lamp fading. "I know what you're about and it won't work, I tell you. I rang that bell."

For one hundred years, princes and noblemen had sounded the bell with love in their hearts. Tonight was his night. His declaration. For Lady Charlene. He'd not be robbed by his so-called best friend.

Michael's heart thudded as he descended, catching himself with each slick step, but as he rounded a curve, a sharp blow cracked against his head. Stumbling against the wall, Michael winced against the pain, trying to stay upright. "Paulson . . ."

"Dare I repeat myself? We are at war, Mick." Paulson leaned into him, his lantern raised. "I will be the first man through the chapel door—"

"Out of my way, chap." With an exhale, Michael smashed his fist against Paulson's chin, the larger man bending forward, absorbing the blow with a soft "umph."

But it was enough. Michael dashed round him but found no traction on the slick stone. He slipped, falling, flailing . . .

The railing . . . if he could reach the railing . . .

His fingers grazed past the old, dried wood. Reaching, Michael at last grabbed hold, his hands sliding against the grain, splinters digging into his skin. When he stopped, he drew his first pure breath and pulled himself upright.

"Paulson, shall we call a truce?" Michael started down the steps, searching the deep shadows for his mate.

But the stone betrayed him again. His boot slipped. Then a slight shove from behind sent him tumbling and he crashed sideways against the unworthy railing. The lumber cracked beneath the force of his weight.

The haunting sound of splintering wood filled his ears. His chest pounded as he toppled headfirst, 182 steps into the black hollow of the Pembroke Chapel tower.

CHAPTER 1

November, Present Day
St. Simons Island, Georgia

If she closed her eyes, she could pretend nothing had changed at the Rib Shack since Daddy died.

Not the click and clack of dishes, the hum of the dishwasher, the sizzle of the fry vat, Bristol barking commands at the window, Catfish singing "Nobody Knows the Trouble I've Seen" while Mama, the queen of the Shack, admonished him to knock it off or he'd see a new kind of trouble.

Catfish just tipped his head back and sang a little louder.

Avery laughed at their exchange, yet still aware of the void made in her chest when her hero left this earth way too soon.

Barely sixty when Daddy's heart said it'd had enough. Nothing was the same without him. Not the Shack, not home, not Mama, not life. For Avery, to say she missed him was more than mere words.

She missed him at the fryer telling Mama to leave him alone. Missed him at the prep counter making his famous barbecue sauce. Missed his wise answers to her anxious questions.

Worse than not being the same, *everything* had changed. Even *she* had changed. She was unsure of herself, of her future, of her very thoughts.

Mama changed the most. The spunk left her soul. Day by day, her bold confidence leaked away. She moved slower, talked lower, cared less.

"Avery?" Mama paused in front of her, flour-stained hands on her aproned waist. "You never said how your doc appointment went."

"Good." Avery touched her shoulder without much thought. "The doc said I'm healing well."

"But your playing days are over?" Mama cut a glance at the new waitress. "LuEllen, just put those dishes by the dishwasher. I'll run them through. Get on back to the dining room."

"I can load the dishwasher, Mama." Avery started around the prep table but Mama gently clasped her arm.

"Answer my question."

She met Mama's eyes, her own bubbling up with tears. "Yes, my playing days are over. At least my competitive playing days."

"So no chance at the beach volleyball circuit?"

Just hearing Mama say it, the words she refused to say herself, inspired tears. Avery shook her head as she ducked away from Mama.

As Big Ten Player of the Year in women's volleyball, her future had been hers to command. At six feet and a strong outside hitter, Avery's professional career was calling.

She'd had an agent. For a moment or two. And the interest of Olympic beach champion Ella Watson.

But the rotator cuff she damaged during her junior season came back to haunt her during her senior-year NCAA championships. Surgery followed with the doctor's stern declaration, *"You're done."*

"How's that sitting with you?" Mama didn't mind pressing into other people's business but threw up brick walls when folks inquired intimate things about her.

"I don't know." Avery moved to the dishwasher and started loading, swallowing a small rise of emotion that felt like it had more to do with Daddy than the end of her volleyball days. "Scary, I guess. Volleyball has been my life for thirteen years. Now what?"

Two summers in a row she toured with a select collegiate team throughout Europe, stopping in Brighton Kingdom to visit her sister, HRH Princess Susanna of Brighton Kingdom, married to King Nathaniel II. That went over well with her starry-eyed teammates.

"You get on with your life, that's what." Mama ran a dish towel through her hands. A nervous habit she picked up after Daddy died. "I could use you around here now that your daddy's gone." She said it so matter-of-factly. So final. *Daddy's gone.*

"Mama, the Shack? Really?" She'd die a young, tragic death if life saddled her to the Rib Shack the rest of her life.

No doubt the family restaurant was her second home. She grew up in the shadows of the lowboy and a deep fryer and had fun doing so. Her childhood memories were to be treasured.

But she had dreams. Of grabbing hold of life. Making a difference in the world. Volleyball had been her conduit. But with that door closed, her slate of dreams toppled to the ground.

And with Daddy not here to guide her.

Avery smiled at LuEllen as she brought around another tray of dishes to be loaded, then turned to Mama. "She seems to be working out well."

Mama glanced over her shoulder. "LuEllen? Yes, she's a hard worker. Avery, darling, easy with those plates. They're sturdy but still made of clay."

Yes, made of clay. Like Mama. Like Avery.

"I was thinking about coaching." Avery loaded the last plate and flipped on the machine.

Mama sighed. "Well, you'd be good. Daddy always said you could do whatever you put your mind to, Aves. But I sure would miss you around here."

"Yeah, but the plan never was for me to make a life here." Avery glanced over at Mama. She stood at the prep table, making biscuits, a mantle of sadness on her shoulders. It happened the day she spread Daddy's ashes over the Atlantic with Avery and Susanna.

"Yeah, well, my darling, life has a way of turning the tide on you."

"Tell you what," Avery said, moving Mama aside. "Why don't you go on home? You've been here since the crack of dawn. Take the rest of the afternoon off. Rest. I don't think you've had a day off since tourist season picked up."

"I'd rather work." Mama didn't budge. Avery understood. She felt the same way. Work kept her distracted, away from self-pity. Away from a home without Daddy's light.

"You could go on home, though," Mama said. "Rest your shoulder. See if those new shutters I paid Bill Springer to put up are done. I tell you, there's no excuse for sloppy service."

But Avery didn't want to go home either. It was dark and lonely, a hollow shell of what it used to be—full of life and laughter, Daddy and Mama's pretend bickering, Susanna coming and going. Until she married a king.

"I think I'd rather work too."

Mama drew a slow, deep inhale. "You've been a rock to me these past six months, Aves. Putting your life on hold to help me out." She shook her head. "I had to get used to Susanna being gone, off to college, then four thousand miles away in Brighton, being a princess and all. Then I sent you off to college, to a Yankee school, no less, to become a volleyball star. Now I have to get used to—" Her words broke, a soft sob escaping her pinched lips.

"I miss him too." Avery put her arms around Mama, who remained stiff, hovering over the prep table, her fist clinched.

"I just . . ." Mama pounded the table. "I just can't get used to it all." She raised her head, wiping her cheeks with the back of her hand. "But, oh, wasn't your daddy proud of you?" Mama returned to the biscuit dough. "He busted his apron strings talking about you. Can't tell you how many times I found him in the old man corner of the Shack with Boss, Duke, and the boys telling them you were Big Ten Player of the Week again, or player of the year, whichever it was . . ." Her voice trailed off. "But I suppose I told you these stories."

"I like hearing them again." Avery tried to see Mama's face, but she kept her shoulder cocked around so she couldn't get a good look. So she wandered over to the sink for a clean damp cloth to wipe down the prep counter. The stories of Daddy filled the holes in her heart. She always knew he was proud of her, but he kept his personal thoughts close to his chest.

Funny, though, the last thing he ever said to her was about love, about Prince Colin. She sighed. No use going down that *very* dead-end road.

"We're going to be fine, Avery-girl, just fine." Mama's declaration wobbled. "The good Lord doesn't forget His own, does He?"

"No, He doesn't." At least that was Avery's conviction if not her experience. Though could she truly point to a time God forgot her?

"Glo?"

Mama glanced around at Catfish, chief cook and bottle washer, as she liked to call him. He was long and lean with thin, scraggly whiskers. Like a catfish.

"Phone. It's Susanna."

"Goodness, I didn't even hear it ring." Mama snatched Avery's damp cloth and wiped her hands as she disappeared into the office, her voice shrill and exuberant as she greeted her eldest daughter. "Susanna, what in the world . . . How are you?"

"Catfish," Avery said, "I'll be back. Taking five."

He waved his reply, head down over the fry vats. Outside on the back deck, Avery slid onto one of the picnic tables, retrieving her phone from her pocket, checking e-mail.

She'd not said anything to Mama yet but she'd applied for a few coaching jobs nearby. Valdosta State, Jacksonville State, and Appalachian State.

If she couldn't play herself, she wanted to coach others.

Then this morning a friend e-mailed her about an opening on the men's team at UCLA. Why not? Men have been coaching women's teams forever. So she applied. *California, here I come.* The Golden State was a long way from home, but she needed change, needed to shed her grave clothes, breathe in life and adventure.

Through the palmettos and pine trees, Avery stared down the path to the beach, where the Atlantic knocked waves against the sand. She'd sat here a million times, but today she felt like a sojourner, a stranger to her own life.

This was all so reminiscent of four years ago when she sat on this same table, in pain, trying to glue together her shattered heart.

She'd already accepted a scholarship to Ohio State so she had a path to follow, something to do. But nothing felt right. She cried herself to sleep. Cried herself awake.

The cool saline breeze swept across the deck and Avery breathed in as the memory, the feelings, surfaced.

She'd been right here, weeks away from her eighteenth birthday, her senior prom, and graduating. Months away from college. *If* she went at all.

Because the preceding winter and spring, she'd fallen in love. In deep, heart-stealing love. Dreams she'd never dreamed before suddenly came true.

But that night—Avery shivered, running her hand along her arm. That night a fresh spring breeze brushed her cheek as she sipped a tall Diet Coke, waiting. Waiting for *him* to call. The one who stole her heart with a single glance.

When her phone buzzed in her hand, it wasn't a call but a text.

COLIN: I can't come.

AVERY: Why? Is everything all right?

COLIN: I just can't. Obligations and all.

AVERY: I'll come to you. I don't need to go to prom. I'd rather be with you.

Colin: No. You go. You're on the court. I'm tied up with studies, exams, prepping for the Royal Navy.

"Aves—" The screen door clapped behind Mama's voice. "Pack your bags. We're going to Brighton Kingdom for Christmas." Mama hopped onto the picnic table next to Avery, brushing her wild curly hair away from her face.

"What?" Avery tucked her phone away, puzzled but liking the lilt in Mama's voice. "Leave the Rib Shack over the holidays?"

Mama never left the restaurant, especially during the Christmas season. Well, once. When Susanna was home from college and Daddy surprised her with tickets to Vermont. She'd never seen snow. So Daddy put Susanna and Avery in charge and dragged Mama to romantic Stow where they were flat out going to have a good time, daggumit.

"Your sister is pregnant again." Mama clapped her knee.

"Really?" Susanna had been trying for three years to produce an heir to the Brighton throne. Avery couldn't imagine the pressure.

"Almost thirteen weeks. She's hopeful. Believing she's not going to lose this one." Susanna had lost five babies in three years, breaking all their hearts each time. "Wouldn't your daddy be shouting to the heavens with this news?" Mama popped Avery on the knee. "So what do you say? Brighton Kingdom for Christmas." She spoke it all in one breath. Like she had to say it before she changed her mind.

"Mama, you do realize Susanna is not going to have the baby next month?"

"Don't get smart with me, Avery Mae. This is the first good news we've had in six months and, shoot-dogs, why not go to Brighton for Christmas? It bothers me that your daddy always wanted to go but I refused, said the Shack needed us over the holidays." Mama raised her left leg, pulling up her pant leg, revealing the marks of decades on her feet. "I've been slaving away in this joint for thirty years and how do I get repaid? Varicose veins and gnarly feet."

"You're really going to leave? Let Catfish and Bristol mind the store while you and I head over to Brighton?" Avery was dubious. "I don't believe it."

Mama popped her hands together, hopping off the picnic table. "Believe it, darling, because we're going to Brighton. I'm going to spend Christmas in a palace, praying over that baby in the womb.

Just think, my grandchild a prince or princess. How about that? Besides, it occurred to me we should spend this Christmas, of all Christmases, together as a family. Gib would want it that way."

Avery slipped off the picnic table and headed back to the kitchen. "You'll worry about the Shack the entire time."

"Nope, done made up my mind. I'm not going to worry." Mama trailed Avery through the kitchen door, straightening as she went, stacking a used biscuit tray by the dishwasher, all automatic moves, the Rib Shack being so much a part of her nature. "We'll leave after Thanksgiving 'cause that ornery sister of mine has the whole family coming here for dinner. But we'll arrive in Cathedral City just in time for that shindig they have every fall." Mama snapped her fingers, facing Avery. "What do they call it?"

"The Harvest Celebration."

"That's it. Won't that be fun? The end of the harvest and the start of the Christmas season. Good-bye farming and hello birth of Jesus."

Avery grinned. Nothing like a Georgia woman to break down an ancient European country's traditions into farming and birthing.

Mama looped her arm around Avery's shoulder. "What do you say, kiddo? You and me to Brighton. I dare say you could use a change of scene. Get out of Dodge, Aves. See how the rest of the world lives. Get a new perspective."

Avery regarded her mother. She wouldn't deny her, not after the year she'd had. Besides, she loved Christmas in Brighton Kingdom. It was about the most magical place on earth—full of tradition, ancient architecture mixed with sterile modern works, snow-covered hills, starlight and sea phosphorous converging on a moonless night, creating an ethereal glow around the North Sea emerald isle known as Brighton Kingdom.

But there was the matter of him. Prince Colin. She didn't want there to be a matter, not after four and a half years, but by the twist in her heart at every mention of Brighton Kingdom there was clearly a matter.

Avery had visited Brighton two Christmases ago, but the navy had shipped Colin out to sea so she didn't have to deal with seeing him.

"Well, I best get back to making biscuits." Mama started for the prep table with a lightness in her step, then paused. "Look at me." She held out her hand. "I'm shaking. I've never traveled without your daddy before." The commander of the USS Rib Shack showed a weakness. One she hid within the love of her husband of thirty-four years.

Avery had always suspected Glo Truitt hated being alone.

"I'll be with you, Mama," Avery said. "Don't worry."

"Of course, of course. Who's worried?" But the tint in her eye said, "Thank you." "Catfish, Bristol, team meeting when we close up." Mama turned for her office. "Avery, tell you what, you make the biscuits. I got a few phone calls to make."

Mama was fired up now. But good. A trip to Brighton, seeing Susanna, experiencing Cathedral City during the holidays settled in Avery like a light in a window.

Brighton meant more than silly ole Prince Colin. In fact, that lovely place meant a lot of things to the Truitts. Family. Love. The unexpected! Oh, especially the unexpected.

First her sister falling for a prince turned king. Watching her walk down the aisle to marry the man she loved amid pomp and circumstance. Avery knew then the impossible was only hindered by doubt and fear.

But the true unexpected that year was Prince Colin, how he

captured her, sweeping her away like she never thought possible. At seventeen, she was gone, simply gone in love. She'd have married him if he'd asked.

At the prep counter, Avery rolled out more dough and reached for the cutter, flipping the thick, round, raw biscuits onto the tray, a familiar, comforting routine.

Brighton also stood for unexpected heartbreak. The love she had for Colin did not turn out for her like Susanna's love for Nathaniel.

This Christmas marked five years since she met him, her prince, cousin to the king, when she and Susanna traveled to Brighton for Nathaniel's coronation.

Then for five months they were young lovers. Not even the four thousand miles between them could quell their affection. Overnight, he became her best friend.

Thinking of him roused a dull pain, and it bothered her that after all this time he still had some power over her. But she must command her emotions.

Surely Colin had moved on. She didn't know for sure because she avoided the grocery store gossip rags and never asked Susanna about him, but he was too much of a catch to be left alone.

She'd thought she'd moved on too. Yet the thought of spending a month—a whole month—in Brighton Kingdom brought it all back again.

Lord, please let the navy ship him out to sea again.

Avery carried the biscuit tray to the convection oven, set the timer, then pressed out the screen door. "Catfish, I'll be back." Leaving the deck, she took the path through the pines and palmettos to the beach.

The moonlight caught the calm ocean surface, taunting her,

inviting her to walk on water. If she squinted her eyes, it seemed she could follow the white path northeast, all the way to Brighton.

Avery inched toward the water, the waves crashing around her feet, pulling the sand out from under her. She'd better get hold of her heart, of her thinking, before traveling. She'd be a mess otherwise.

But for the moment, she breathed out and let her raw, real emotions admit the truth. The one thing that had not changed since Daddy died.

She was still very much in love with Prince Colin of Brighton Kingdom.

CHAPTER 2

Brighton Kingdom

In the wings of the *Madeline & Hyacinth Live!* show, Prince Colin took a last swig of water. Perspiration ran along the collar of his knit pullover.

He'd ridden a naval vessel through a storm and not been as anxious. Because weathering the wind and waves was about his men, his crew, all hands on deck with each one doing his part.

The Maddie and Hy show was all eyes on him.

"Two minutes, Your Highness." The stage manager flashed his hand past Colin's eyes.

"Please, I'm not 'Your Highness.'" His voice croaked and cracked, the stage manager moving on, not listening. "I'm not an HRH," Colin muttered to himself.

If no one else cared, he cared. It was an honor to be His Royal Highness. Colin's status was of a mere prince. A title fought for and won by his father.

A member of the Brighton royal family, fifth in line to the Stratton throne, Colin was more than happy to do his part when his cousin, King Nathaniel II, asked him to appear on the national afternoon talk show.

There weren't two more popular presenters in all of Brighton and the Grand Duchy of Hessenberg than Madeline and Hyacinth. The King's Office claimed the women had the pulse of popular culture.

Colin was here to talk about the Christmas season and upcoming events, one especially near and dear to his heart, but he felt infinitely more comfortable in his father's boardroom, or playing sports, or hunting, or riding the seas in a royal naval vessel than representing the family on national telly.

From his jacket pocket, his phone buzzed. It was his father's assistant, texting.

Your dad says "Break a leg, son."

Colin breathed in, then slowly exhaled, grinning. Dad, a tycoon of business, did not own a cell phone. He worked religiously from an iPad, but he did not text. If you wanted to get in touch with Edward Tattersall, you must employ good old-fashioned e-mail.

Dad's pride encouraged and terrified Colin. His father's belief in him got him through grammar school bullying. He taught Colin how to stand up for himself, throw a good punch. Dad's guidance led Colin through university and the royal naval command school.

Dad was his hero. The one person he could never let down. It haunted him.

If it weren't for Dad, Colin would not even be a royal, which meant he wouldn't be standing here now, sweating it out. Royalty came with its, um, privileges.

"Five seconds, Prince Colin," the stage manager said as he passed by.

Colin peeked around the edge of the curtain backstage. Madeline and Hyacinth faced the camera and the rather large audience, smiling.

"Ladies and gentlemen, we are so excited about our next guest."

Colin's blood rushed under his skin. The makeup tech dashed toward him, blotting his face, whisking him with a translucent powder.

"Try not to perspire so much."

"I'll give it a go."

But he was dubious. The main stage was flooded with hot lights. And every eye in the studio and across Brighton would be on him.

"Please, give a big Madeline and Hyacinth welcome to first-time guest—"

"But we hope he'll be back!"

"Prince Colin."

He darted forward from the shadows into the glaring lights, pressing against the force of mostly female applause, shouts, and whistles.

"Welcome, welcome!" Madeline greeted him with a kiss, then Hyacinth.

Nothing but a ship at sea, nothing but a ship at sea . . . Colin sat in the high director's chair between the TV presenters, forcing his nerves aside, digging deep on his training, finding his confidence.

He caught his face in the monitor. He was smiling. And thankfully, not drenched in sweat.

"It's so good to have you." Madeline tapped his knee with her notes. "Why has it taken so long to get you on the show?"

"You've been too infatuated with Nathaniel and Stephen, but yes, thanks for having me."

The audience laughed and he breathed out a little.

"Oh, listen to you. Calling us out," Hyacinth said.

Colin sat back, locking his hands over the end of the chair's arms. *Relax, you're a seasoned sailor. A prince of business if not this royal kingdom.* His father would say, "You are your father's son!"

"Listen, so let's talk about all the great things going on during the Christmas season at the palace and around the city." Madeline was the serious one of this two-ring circus.

"Like the children's night at the palace," Hyacinth said. "Your uncle, Prince Aris, is playing St. Nicholas, right?"

"Prince Aris?" Colin feigned surprise. "Not at all. We have on good authority the real St. Nick will be at the palace to see the children." He winked at Hyacinth, who nodded, going along. "But I'll be there. The children are lovely to be around."

"Oh, Maddie, I think my heart just melted." Hyacinth, with her smoldering voice and diva good looks, flipped her long hair over her shoulder.

Colin didn't need the monitor to know his cheeks flushed a royal red.

"Stop, you're embarrassing him," Madeline said. "Since your cousin Prince Stephen's marriage to American heiress Corina Del Rey, you are the nation's most eligible bachelor."

Madeline and Hyacinth were obsessed with naming Brighton's most eligible bachelor. "Don't know about most eligible—"

"I know, that's all wrong," Madeline said. "More like you're the most desirable."

Now he laughed. "Definitely not. You can ask my mum about how tidy I am not."

"Well, you can come mess up my house any day." Hyacinth turned to the camera. "Don't get too riled up, ladies. Our prince here is dating a Brighton actress, the stunning Lady Jordan Skye, whose latest romantic comedy, *Before Us There Was Me*, became a box office hit."

"So, is it love for you two?" Madeline arched her brow, so keen in her prying.

The King's Office had warned him Madeline and Hyacinth went for the personal jugular.

"We get on well," he said.

"Marriage?"

Ah yes, here comes the obvious perspiring. "Are you proposing to me, Hyacinth?"

The audience gasped, then roared as Hyacinth sat back, her cheeks blushing.

"Hyacinth, he caught you flat." Madeline offered Colin a high five. "He's crafty, this one. So let's talk about the great Brighton Christmas traditions, many of them right here in our capital, Cathedral City."

The show presenters moved to familiar, steady ground. Marriage was a touchy subject with him. He'd not even broached the topic with Jordan. Which seemed to please her. After all, he was only twenty-six. She'd just turned twenty-eight, and her career was taking off.

If they were to be married, there was gobs of time.

"Christmas is the royal family's favorite time of year," Colin said, finding it easy to speak from the heart. "A time we love to give to the people, carry out old traditions."

His favorite thing about being a royal was his position to help others. To be a voice and an advocate. "We want to encourage everyone to come out for all the public events. If you're running an event in your borough or dell, please send notice to the King's Office. They'll pop it on the Christmas website straightaway."

Madeline pointed to the green screen behind her. "Here's a list of the upcoming events . . . Caroling in the downtown square, Christmas movie Sunday afternoon and evening at the Royal Sundown Theatre, free admission. The palace Christmas Extravaganza for children under ten . . . be sure to register your children at your local school." She leaned to Colin. "And of course the Christmas Symphony, which we know is a Tattersall family tradition."

"Indeed."

"And the highlight of the season, the Christmas Ball on the twenty-eighth, the most exciting and sad night of the season. A glorious ball but the end of the holiday."

"But then it's on to the new year." Colin smiled at the audience, encouraging their applause. New Year's was a quiet time for Brightonians, having put all their energies into Christmas. Most people held small parties with friends and family.

"We are so excited about the new year," Hyacinth said. "We will be hosting Brighton's first televised New Year's Eve party. We're going to be downtown in Leopold Hall and it should be smashing. Everyone, please come out and bring in the new year with us."

"But the big news for today is Prince Colin's organization, one he patrons with Princess Susanna, the Earn-A-Pound-Buy-A-Gift," Madeline read from the teleprompter. "Children will be at Maritime Park selling their creations to earn money for Christmas gifts."

Finally, the real reason he agreed to do this show. "This is a great charity. Studies have shown people are more likely to have pride in themselves when they can purchase gifts with money they've earned. So we are hosting a children's fair in Maritime Park where they can sell the things they've made in an afterschool program to earn gift money for their families."

A hearty applause rippled through the audience.

"I'm really excited about this," Madeline said. "You did a test program at a school last year with huge success."

"Indeed, we did. This year we decided to take it city wide. Next year we'll go to more cities and schools."

"That's so fantastic. What's your favorite part of the fair?"

"Seeing the children's faces when they count up their money at the end of the day. One lad earned five hundred pounds with his skillfully crafted skateboards last year. Rupert. I'll never forget him. And for all the pounds earned, our family matches it. So it's all around a good day."

"We'll be at Market Square next weekend, won't we, Maddie?" Hyacinth encouraged the crowd and they responded. Colin wanted to slip out of his chair and preach to them.

This is what Christmas is all about!

"Of course, we open the Christmas season with the Harvest Celebration," Hyacinth said. "Cities across the kingdom will be hosting dances and parties, saying good-bye to fall and the hard work of harvest, an age-old tradition in Brighton. I love this celebration. It ushers in the Christmas season so perfectly. Prince Colin, will the royal family be dancing at the palace?"

"Of course. It's tradition. I'm looking forward to it."

"Will Lady Jordan be there?"

Clever. Madelyn brought the conversation back round to his personal life. He laughed, relaxing a bit, getting the rhythm of these two experienced presenters. "She'll be there."

"Well, that being said . . ." Hyacinth reached for a card tucked under her leg, waving it in the air. "Our staff did a bit of digging and we found an old tradition no one has talked about in years. I faintly remember my granny bringing it up." She faced the audience. "Do any of you remember the tradition of the Pembroke Chapel bell?"

The audience generated a slight applause. Colin made a face, feigning disinterest. Where was she going with this? Because he knew the old chapel well.

Though hardly a chapel now—only the bell tower remained after World War II. What remained sat on the back lawn of the palace. He was surprised Nathaniel's father, Uncle Leo, didn't have the eyesore torn down during his reign.

"Prince Colin, do you know about this tradition? It does herald from royals and aristocrats." Hyacinth waited for his reply.

He shrugged. "Something about ringing the bell at midnight of the Harvest Celebration."

Whatever the tradition used to be, Colin and his mates had a tradition of their own at Pembroke—pipes and pints at one minute past the hour. They escaped the party and the perfume just before the stroke of midnight, scurried to the tower, and carefully climbed the slick stone stairs to the top.

They looked out over the city, talking about the night, their goals, what the year had wrought. What the new year might bring.

But the bell? They avoided that thing like the Black Death.

Madeline faced the audience, speaking with flair and animation. "As the story goes, the first prince to ring the bell for his true love was in 1734. For a hundred years the tradition continued."

Behind them, artist renderings of the princes and noblemen racing the tower steps illustrated the story.

"Until Prince Michael in 1834. He was in love with Lady Charlene and chose tradition on the night of the Harvest Celebration to declare his feelings. He ran up the 182 steps of the chapel tower at midnight and rang the bell loud and long at one minute past midnight, just as the city's cathedral bells fell silent. Then he set off to win his true love and marry her Christmas Day in Watchman Abbey."

"However"—Hyacinth took up the story—"He slipped and fell to his death, landing on the cold, stone tower floor. His mate, Lord Paulson Wetherby, witnessed the whole thing. It's claimed he was never the same afterward."

"Since then, no man has attempted the tower steps again, nor the ringing of the bell."

Madeline and Hyacinth glared at Colin.

"Don't look at me." He shifted in his seat. "There's a reason no man has run those slick, smooth steps in a century plus. The death of Prince Michael."

Madeline faced the camera with the glowing red light. "It's time for the bell to ring again. Is there some brave chap who dares the 182 steps? To win the heart of his true love in twenty-four days to marry her on Christmas Day at Watchman Abbey?"

Hyacinth began a slow, low chant. "Prince Colin, Prince Colin, Prince Colin . . ."

"No, no, whoa, not me. Don't do that to a chap." He slapped his hand to his chest. "I'm just out of the navy, in a new job with my father. Isn't it time we go to a commercial?"

Madeline encouraged the chant until his chest churned with the rhythm of the dirge, threatening the secrets of his heart.

Then Hyacinth sat forward. "It's been 182 years since a prince rang the bell?" She held up her cue cards. "And there are

182 steps to the top?" She shivered, and under her makeup her skin paled. "That's weird."

"I've goose bumps." Madeline ran her hand up and down her arm.

"It's a sign."

Colin winced, caught between the vibe of the women. It wasn't a sign. At least not for him. He liked Lady Jordan a lot—Lady Jay to her close friends—but he was not in love with her. There were times when he wondered if he'd ever be in love again.

Where did a man go after giving up the love of his life?

"This is giving me the willies," Hyacinth said to the camera. "We're going to think on it while we take a break. We'll be back with more of Prince Colin."

The lights went down and the cameras faded back.

"You're doing great," Madeline said, stepping away from her chair. The audience settled down, reaching for their phones, taking snapshots of Colin and the set.

Someone handed Colin a bottle of water. The makeup tech appeared, patting his face and dusting him again with powder.

"You're doing good. Try to sweat just a little less."

"The lights are hot."

She winked at him. "So's the conversation."

Colin grimaced, watching her leave, taking a swig of his water. He'd not be bullied into ringing a bell, or proposing to a girl he didn't love.

Besides, lasses today could not be expected to marry any man in twenty-four days at the country's most prestigious abbey. He had two younger sisters, and if he had learned anything about women and weddings, the nuptials had to be on the bride's terms.

Next to him, Hyacinth remained unmoved. "Is it weird? We

bring up this tradition 182 after Prince Michael falls to his death? And there are exactly 182 steps from the bottom to the top." She shivered again. "I feel like I've touched something beyond the veil."

Colin sipped his water. "If you ask me, it's superstition. There's nothing to it. Just a coincidence."

"You ever been in the chapel tower?" Hyacinth motioned for him to follow her to the other side of the set. They were going to demonstrate Harvest Celebration dances and reels.

"A few times." Colin didn't want to give away his secret to this media diva. She'd probably announce it to the entire kingdom after the break.

"Ever think of ringing the bell?"

"Never."

The presenter smiled. "I don't blame you. You're young. Live a little." She winked. "But I had to do my bit of prying for the show, you know."

"And I have to do my bit and deny everything."

"Ha, so true, love, so true."

Oddly, Dad had been trumpeting marriage recently. *"Isn't it time?"* Mum joined Dad's hinting, already preparing a place for Jordan at Christmas dinner.

"I've heard the steps to the chapel are slick as winter ice," Hyacinth said. "I'd never run them."

"I've heard the same." Colin knew full well they were slick, round with time and dripping rain water, but he and the lads managed.

A few years ago his mate Guy Smoot nearly fell to his peril. The railing had been repaired since Prince Michael's demise, but it was worn and thirsty from a new set of days and decades. Guy was able to catch himself just in time.

Perhaps they'd had a pint too many. The incident sobered them. Colin curbed his youthful imbibing afterward.

"A chap would have to be head over heels in love to ring that bell with his intended unaware," Hy said. "Then woo her and marry her by Christmas."

"Braver soul than I," Colin said.

"You ever been head over heels, Prince Colin?" She leaned into him. "Lady Jay is gorgeous, but I don't see 'I'm wild about her' in your eyes."

He'd underestimated Hyacinth. "Does anyone understand love?"

"Precisely. That's what I keep telling Maddie."

The stage manager called, "Back in one . . ."

But Hyacinth's question resonated through Colin. Had he ever been head over heels? Indeed. Once. A long time ago. Nearly five years now. With a girl who was a world away. A different man loved her than the one about to demonstrate a traditional Brighton reel on the *Madeline & Hyacinth Live!* show.

He'd been a young, carefree college chap named Colin Tattersall who was completely unprepared to fall so passionately in love with Avery Truitt.

But his father helped him to see his folly. Colin was a man of destiny, one with obligations, responsibilities, and plans he'd worked on with Dad for years. Since joining the family firm, he needed to focus now more than ever. This was not a season for love.

Someday a chap might ring the Pembroke bell again. Who knew? But sure as his name was Colin Edward Stratton Tattersall, a prince in Brighton Kingdom, he knew it wasn't going to be him.

CHAPTER 3

R emember the first time we arrived in Cathedral City?"

Avery turned to see Susanna at her door, gliding across the room wearing a Jenny Packham gown, her hair piled on top of her head in smooth, glistening curls, a diamond tiara woven in.

"You rolled down the window and hung out of the car." With a soft laugh, Susanna sat on a bedroom chair, her skirt flowing over the red cushions. "Seems like forever ago."

Avery watched her sister through the vanity mirror where Susanna's stylist, Natasha, worked her curling iron like a magic wand through Avery's long reddish tresses.

A true princess, Susanna. Born on St. Simons Island but destined for the island of Brighton Kingdom.

"Head up please, miss," Natasha said.

"Suz, did you imagine you'd marry Nathaniel? Really?" The whirlwind St. Simons Island romance seemed doomed when Nathaniel confessed that his royal status prevented him from marrying a foreigner.

"I wasn't even sure I'd see him again. I wanted to marry him, you know I did." Susanna sat forward, her long slender arms crossed over her legs. "You look beautiful, Avery."

"Feels funny being all dressed up." She glanced down at her dress of brown velvet held wide by layers of blue chiffon and white tulle. Natasha grabbed the side of her head, tipping her straight again. "I'm so used to being on the volleyball court or in the Shack's kitchen."

"Or surfing."

"Well, yes, surfing." Avery smiled. The waves and wind of the Atlantic were her lullaby. "Where did you find this dress? It's gorgeous."

"Melinda House. It's a vintage remake of a fifties Christian Dior. When I saw it I thought of you. The brown is gorgeous with your auburn hair. Perfect colors for the Harvest Celebration."

Mama entered, her hair in hot rollers, knocking the life out of an off-the-shoulder burnt-orange organza gown.

"Mama!" Avery whistled, watching her mother through the mirror. "You look . . . not at all like my mama."

"Miss, please, we're almost done." Natasha raised Avery's head with her vice grip.

"I clean up all right for a gal who's been in a kitchen for more years than I care to remember." Mama made a slow turn. "I think I'm rocking this dress, as they say."

Avery laughed. "Listen to you. My mama the hipster."

"Whatever that means." Mama leaned over Avery's shoulder. "You look lovely, darling. Now, you're both expected in my suite post haste. Rollins is bringing tea to my room."

"Tea in your suite? Post haste?" Avery made a face, exchanging smiles with Susanna. Mama drank her morning coffee on the run. And she never said post haste.

"Well, when living in a palace, act like a royal. It'll be pots and pans and deep frying soon enough. I'm off to let my lady's maid finish my hair." Mama backed toward the door, trying a Brighton accent, miming a sip of tea with her pinky in the air. "Aren't I something?"

"She's not a lady's maid, Mama," Susanna called after her. "She's a stylist the palace hires for special events."

Too late. Mama was gone.

Natasha released the last of Avery's hair from the curling iron, letting it fall over her shoulder. She leaned to see Avery in the mirror. "There. Look at you with your Audrey Hepburn neck. What do you think, ma'am?" Natasha turned to Susanna.

"I think my sister is quite beautiful."

"Then I'm off." The stylist gathered her things. "I'll go help Leslie with the queen and check in on His Majesty. Have a darling good time tonight."

"Thank you, Natasha." Susanna stood as the front room door clicked closed. "Avery, how's Mama? Really?"

"Different. Subdued. But since we've been here, she's the liveliest I've seen her since he died."

"She doesn't really know what to do without Daddy. All that fake bickering hid how much they loved and depended on one another."

"What about you, Suz? You okay?" Avery slipped on the matching shrug and smoothed her hands over the fanning skirt. She did love a gorgeous dress.

"Doing well, though it's hard being so far away. Nathaniel helped me walk through it. He still misses his dad." Her hand moved to her belly and gently rested there. "This little one helps."

"Are you afraid about losing this one?" Avery slipped her arm through her sister's. "Let's pool our faith and believe everything will be all right."

Susanna's eyes glistened. "We pray every night for this baby. But yes, let's pool our faith." She kissed her sister's cheek. "I'm so glad you came into the world. You were like this living, breathing, brown-eyed, redheaded baby doll to me." She grinned, pinching Avery's cheek. "Who grew into an enormous pest."

"Hey now. Only because I wanted to be like you." Avery laughed, heading toward the front room. "And if you think I was a pest, wait until this baby comes."

"Bring it, sista." But the humor in Susanna's voice didn't reflect in her eyes. Instead, Avery saw a somberness there. "We've been married almost five years. I've been pregnant five times and lost every one. It's starting to feel like a bad habit."

"Not this time." Avery picked up the clutch Melinda House sent over to go with the dress and stuffed it with a piece of gum, ChapStick, and her favorite lip gloss. "I can feel it."

"Unfortunately, I feel it too. This baby is not just about Nathaniel and me wanting a family. It's about the House of Stratton and producing heirs. The press is crazy with monthly headlines debating our ability to reproduce. As if the 450-year-old dynasty depended on my womb alone. Thank goodness Corina and Stephen are trying too."

Stephen was Nathaniel's younger brother. His wife, Corina, another Georgia girl, believe it or not, was an American heiress who married the spare heir in secret.

"Then relax." Avery looped her arm through Susanna's as they headed toward Mama's suite, down the gilded, ornate hallway framed with carved crown molding and two inches of thick royal burgundy carpet. "God started this, didn't He? Fear and worry won't help. Look at all He's done for you so far. Remember what Daddy always told us? 'He works all things for the good.' He'll see to Nathaniel's heir, Suz. Meanwhile, you live with a man who adores you."

Susanna touched the corner of her eye to keep her tears from spilling. "Listen to you, my wise little sister, expertly doling out advice and spouting Daddyisms."

Avery rested her cheek on Susanna's shoulder. "I miss him. And you."

"I'm sorry it all falls on your shoulders, Aves, to be there for Mama."

"We have a good gig between us, Mama and me. We manage. But when you called saying you were pregnant and invited us over for the Christmas season, I saw a light in her I've not seen since the funeral. She came alive."

"Then let's make this the best Christmas ever."

"Best Christmas ever?" The sisters passed through the prisms of Christmas colors filling the corridor from the wall sconces. "I'm not sure you can beat '06 when all the cousins came and I got a new bike."

"Ooo, good one."

"Or the Christmas of '07 when it snowed—"

"Or what we in southern Georgia called snow."

Avery laughed, loving the swoosh and flair of her skirt against her legs. Loving the swirl of anticipation for the night ahead. A big fancy party with no cares. At least for a few hours.

"But boy, we had fun in '07, didn't we?" She'd not even hinted to Susanna about Colin. Best just let the past stay behind her. Besides, her gut told her he was out to sea. Or stationed abroad. "I tried to make a snowball, but nothing would stick together so I just smashed my wet, slightly-covered-with-white-snow mitten in Marco Hernandez's face."

Susanna laughed. "Makes me homesick."

"But you're getting used to it here, aren't you?"

"I am, and bringing a child into the world"—she hugged her belly tighter—"Will make it feel more like family." Susanna linked her arm tighter with her little sister's. "I hope you find someone like Nathaniel, Avery. Never settle."

"Don't plan on it."

"*Sooo*," Susanna said, slow and full of questions, "four years on that big Ohio State campus and you didn't find someone special?"

"Nope."

"Why do I get the feeling you're not telling me something?" Susanna paused at Mama's door.

"There's nothing to tell." She'd tried dating at Ohio State, but where does a girl land when her first love was her true love? And a prince to boot. "Too busy with school and volleyball."

"But you dated?"

"Sure. Just no one serious." Avery reached for the doorknob. "We'd better get in there or we won't have time for tea."

"Aves—" Susanna grabbed her hand. "About tonight . . . everyone will be at this hootenanny." Their gazes locked for one knowing moment. "All of the family, I mean."

"Well, of course." Avery shrugged off Susanna's insinuation, annoyed by the sudden pounding of her heart. "I'd expect the family to be there."

"Nathaniel insists they are all on deck during December. Starting with the Harvest Celebration through the Christmas Ball on the twenty-eighth." Susanna reached for Avery's hand, squeezing. "It's a lot of fun, really. Have you met his cousin Prince Tony, fourth in line to the throne? He's a blast. His wife, Princess Rachel, is probably my best girlfriend."

"Then I look forward to meeting them." Avery popped a wide smile. "Now can we go in and see what the mighty Glo is doing?" She tried for the door again, but Susanna gripped her hand all the tighter.

"You know he's dating the actress Lady Jordan Skye."

Funny how *he* meant Colin, and they both knew it.

Avery gazed at the floor and the pointed tips of her brown suede sling backs. "I know." She'd braved a Google search one night when she was feeling sentimental, thinking about Christmas in Brighton. A stupid move, really.

"He'll be there with her tonight."

Avery pulled her hand free of Susanna's. "Not my business." She'd always been honest with her sister, always wore her heart on her sleeve, but in the moment it just seemed so ridiculous to bring up her past with the prince. To even hint at lingering feelings. It'd been well over four years, going on five, since their relationship ended. Avery sometimes wondered if it wasn't all some elaborate dream.

"Aves?" Susanna blocked her entrance into Mama's suite. "Talk to me."

"It's just . . . I don't know . . . with Daddy dying and being out of school, off the volleyball court, I feel out of sorts sometimes. And I think too much."

"Do you miss Colin?"

"Not really." Avery turned her back to her sister, staring down the hall toward the light flooding around the corners, keeping a surge of tears at bay. "Why would I miss him? He stood me up the week before my senior prom. Delivered the news to me in a text then never spoke to me again."

"But?" How did Susanna always know there was more?

"It's just that I can't come to Brighton without remembering our first trip here, you know? How Colin was such a fun surprise."

"He was, and you two hit it off instantly."

"I loved him." So she admitted it. Love had a way of wanting to speak.

"And now?" Susanna was relentless.

"It's been years, Suz. Of course I don't love him now." Avery's scoff accented her denial.

"Just checking," Susanna said, smiling. "I think when you see him again, you'll realize you've moved on. Besides, there will be plenty of handsome, available men at the celebration tonight. You won't be a wallflower, trust me."

"Good. I'm looking forward to some fun. I just don't want to appear pathetic to him, you know. New girl at the dance, no one talking to her."

"Won't happen. And you could never look pathetic to him. You're bold and confident. Beautiful. Just be the Avery Truitt who was Big Ten Player of the Year. Twice."

Susanna's truth, while gentle, cauterized any lingering notion that this visit might repeat her first where she caught the eye of lean, aristocratic Prince Colin, a man with an outdoorsman ruddiness, the edge of a salty grin on his lips, and a twinkle that made her insides tumble.

Mama's door swung open. "Land sakes, what're y'all doing out here? The tea's got cold. But never mind. Rollins rang. The security patrol is here." She stepped for the wide, curved staircase, shooing

Susanna and Avery along. "Let's get going. The dowager and Henry are waiting in the foyer."

"I'll meet you there." Susanna broke away, heading on down the corridor. "I'll need to hurry Nathaniel along. King or not, the man is a slowpoke."

"Then it's you and me, Aves."

Alongside Mama, Avery descended the grand staircase, meeting Nathaniel's mama, Queen Campbell, and her husband, a former prime minister, just outside the tall, wide, bulwark palace doors.

Harvest Celebration tradition dictated the royal family walk around the palace's exterior to the grand ballroom, waving to the well-wishers and royal watchers lined along the distant gates.

The security detail and approved members of the press walked along with them, asking questions, snapping photographs.

"What do you think of the festivities, Mrs. Truitt?"

"I'm having a ball." Mama waved to the people as if the queen of Georgia barbecue had rights in Brighton Kingdom.

Avery walked with her head high, a fixed smile on her face, but her thoughts raced forward. Darn it, Susanna, for bringing up Colin. A nervous twist bothered her peace.

The idea of seeing him for the first time since his prom cancelation brought her memories to the forefront. Unlocked her stowed away emotions.

She still loved him. And suddenly her heart remembered just how *much*.

CHAPTER 4

He emerged from the limousine with Lady Jordan on his arm. Cameras flashed, beating back the night. The dull roar of the gathering crowd traveled from the gates to the steps.

Buttoning his tux jacket, Colin aided Jordan as they climbed the steps to the ballroom. Shouts and whistles buoyed in the air.

"Lady Jordan, over here . . ."

"Lady Jordan, we hear you're up for a new movie."

"We shall see." She smiled and flirted, moved like magic, capturing every eye.

She was stunning, no question, with her long, chestnut hair flowing over her bare shoulders, her curves unmistakable in a fitted emerald gown.

The press aimed questions at Colin.

"What are your thoughts on the Brighton Eagles without your cousin, Prince Stephen?"

"Are you two serious? Will there be a royal wedding soon?"

"We saw you on the telly, Prince Colin. Are you going to ring the Pembroke bell?"

Colin waved and smiled, giving no answers as he disappeared with Jordan into the ballroom.

Here was the thing. He liked Jordan. A lot. She was rather down to earth for someone so beautiful, so sought after. But she put him in mind of his sisters' porcelain dolls. Something to sit on a shelf and behold from a distance. She was not one to carry out into life, to cart around the garden and play with in the dirt, to make a go of this thing called love and marriage.

In the ballroom, music rose from the orchestra pit. The violins sang "The Song of Harvest," a Brighton concerto commissioned by King Leo III to celebrate the end of harvest.

With a casual glance around, Colin knew most of the faces. There was his mate Guy Smoot, his partner in Pembroke Chapel mischief. He hoped Madeline and Hyacinth's chatter about the long-dead tradition didn't inspire some poor, weak-minded chap to try to ring the bell for his true love tonight. The questions about it from the media gave him concern.

Colin rather looked forward to his tradition with Guy, standing at the top of the old chapel tower and gazing out over the beautiful Cathedral City, anticipation of Christmas in the air, a good pipe and a tall pint of bitters in their hands.

"Colin," Jordan said, leaning his way, her perfume commanding the air. "I see Lord Wallaby. He's such a patron of film. Let me go over to say hi." She slipped her hand from his arm, but he caught hold of her before she walked off.

"You don't have to be on all the time, Jordan."

"Then you've never worked in the arts." She tossed him a coy glance, more perfect than fun, and left him on the edge of the dance floor.

Couples strolled around and past him, their faces glowing, eager for an evening of frivolity. Every woman was beautiful, every man, dashing.

The three-hundred-year-old Harvest Celebration was one of the many things that made Brighton unique among their European brethren. Celebrating a good harvest, thanking the Lord for His blessings, then rolling right into a monthlong celebration of Christmas.

When he was at sea, Colin missed this time of year the most.

At the far end of the ballroom, Nathaniel sat on the dais with Susanna, leaning close, talking, his hand stroking hers. They commanded the room, those two, and didn't even notice. If he could have what they had . . . one day . . .

The woman next to Susanna glanced up, smiling, waving. Colin frowned. Was she waving at him? She looked familiar but who—

His breath caught. Mrs. Truitt. Avery's mum. He jerked around, scanning the room. Was Avery about? He'd not heard anything of her arrival.

His search paused on every auburn and reddish-brown female head.

"So Lady Jordan?" Guy dug his elbow into Colin's side. "Things are looking rather serious."

Colin turned to his friend. "What?"

"Jordan. You. Serious. Look at you. Can't keep your eyes off her."

"Right, of course . . . Jordan." It didn't appear Avery traveled over with her mum. Good . . . good. He wasn't prepared to see her for the first time since, well . . . he'd ended things. He'd always known this day would come. He simply preferred it not be this day. Nevertheless, a slight disappointment weighted his relief. Colin motioned for Guy to follow. He needed something to drink. His throat was parched. "So, who are you with tonight?"

"Lady Sarah Frizz. Who else?" Guy said with no amount of enthusiasm.

"If you dislike her, why are you here with her? You two bicker like enemies." Ah, a server with a tray of holiday punch. Colin took two cups.

"Dislike? No, my dear chap, the term you're looking for is extreme disdain." Guy took one of the crystal cups from Colin. "But my father loves her and he holds the strings to my future."

"Ah, the money, of course. Smoot, you're a gentleman and a scholar if not a gold digger of your own fortune." Colin gulped from the cup in his right hand. The sudden notion Avery Truitt was in the ballroom turned him into a human desert.

"Do I hear judgment?" Guy raised his punch to someone across the room. "You're no better, leaving that poor American girl in the lurch on her . . . what was it, prom or some such? All because your father didn't approve."

"It's not the same and you know it."

"Ha! I know no such thing. You're as much under your father's control as I. Only I admit it. And I choose to date the women of which he approves. How can I go wrong?"

"My father likes all the women I've dated."

"Except the American." Guy arched his brow, daring Colin to deny him.

"Which was a long time ago." This conversation irritated him. Colin set his empty cup on a passing server's tray and drank from the one in his left hand. Why was Guy bringing up Avery now? Moreover, why was her mother on the dais with Nathaniel?

"Say what you will." Guy clapped Colin on the shoulder. "But we both know we'll marry as our social status demands. And the voice of that status is our fathers' money. In your case, your title as well."

"Don't put me in your class, mate. I rather like and trust my father. He's always been there for me. He'd not stand in the way of true love and my happiness."

The music faded, leaving Colin's reply naked and exposed. He cleared his throat and drained the last of his punch as the lively notes of a Brighton waltz set the dancers in motion.

With a laugh on his lips, Guy disposed of his empty cup. "I dare say your father has already interfered with true love and your happiness." He relieved Colin of his crystal and shoved him toward the dance floor. "But let's leave it be. I came to dance. How about you with Sarah? Me with Jordan?"

Fine. Anything to distract his thoughts from Avery and Guy's observation. Dad stand in the way of true love? Certainly not. He wasn't the sort. He'd moved heaven and earth thirty years ago to marry Mum. Moved the atmosphere once again to gain his son and two daughters their rightful titles as prince and princesses when the king, Uncle Leo, wanted to style them with lesser titles.

"There she is," Guy said, pointing to Lady Sarah.

She spied Colin and smiled. Guy must be mad to despise her. She was beautiful and charming. Also, quite the scholar. She lacked Lady Jordan's sexy sparkle, but how many of those sorts did the world need? Sarah was the sort a man could make a life with.

Moving through the dancers, greeting new and old friends, Colin paused as another mate of his danced past. David Simpson, the recently titled Lord Chrysler after his father's untimely passing, was an old mate. A school chum.

"David, hello—" Colin stopped, catching a glimpse of the woman in David's arms. She was beautiful, by her profile and cut of her jaw. She also looked familiar.

Had he encountered her before? In the summer? Down at the shore with his former naval friends?

A familiar fragrance wafted around him. One that reminded him of warm southern seas. His pulse kicked up. Was it her? He started after David, but Guy clapped his hand on his shoulder.

"Sarah, Prince Colin would be delighted to have this dance." Guy shoved her toward him.

"Stop pushing me, you boorish brute." Sarah jerked from Guy's grasp. "Colin, seriously, how can you stand him?" She snarled at her date. "He's such a cad."

Colin drew his attention from David and the woman with whom he danced, from the fading scent of salty breezes and palmettos, and took Sarah into his arms. "He says he despises you."

"The feeling is mutual." She hollered toward Guy's disappearing back. "Let me guess. He wants to dance with Jordan."

"Doesn't everyone?"

She laughed, a nice solid sound. "I certainly don't." She moved easily to the music, following Colin through the boxy steps. "Who was the woman with David?"

He peered at Sarah. "What?"

"I saw you watching. Sorry, it's the psychiatrist training."

"I don't know. She seemed familiar. Her perfume—"

"Of course. She's probably wearing the new fragrance from D'amond. It's all the rage this season. You'll be sick of it by Christmas. Even I succumbed to its popularity."

But the musky fragrance on Lady Sarah's skin was not the one he had inhaled a few moments ago.

That scent wasn't new to him. It was comfortable. Like arriving home after a long, hard day.

"Tell me, Sarah, why do you hang out with Guy if you hate each other?"

"Ah, the question of the ages. Our parents put us in a crib together when we were two months old. Didn't he ever tell you? The story goes we were so quiet our mums came to check on us. We were fast asleep and Guy was holding my hand."

"So it was meant to be?" Colin moved smoothly with Sarah around the dance floor, one eye on his partner, one eye scanning for David.

"I don't know about that, but I've long suspected he secretly adores me."

Colin laughed. "Sarah, you're already perfect for him."

"And what about you, Prince Colin? Is Lady Jordan the one you adore? Wedding rumors are mounting. Your spot on the *Madeline & Hyacinth Live!* show piqued everyone's curiosity."

"Then they can remain curious. I'm only twenty-six. What do I know of love?"

He'd discussed the matter rather impetuously many times at the Sword & Buckle with his friends but reached no conclusions.

"What do you do if you think you've lost the girl who could be 'the one'?"

The lads had no clue.

Sarah sobered. "I'll say this, Colin, you know what you don't want."

"Do I? Are you using your psychiatrist wiles on me, Sarah?"

"I should say yes, but I'm using my feminine wiles instead."

"Ah, then I'm exposed. Nowhere to hide."

"If you loved Jordan, you'd ring the bell for her. If you loved her, you'd not give Guy Smoot a turn on the dance floor with her."

Colin laughed. "Am I supposed to be that jealous?"

"I'm just saying when a man loves a woman he'll move heaven and earth to be with her."

Colin slowed his steps. "Did I say that to you? Move heaven and earth?" He felt rather exposed. His private thoughts about Dad coming from the lips of Lady Sarah.

"No. Have I touched on something? What? Tell me. There is someone you love. I can see it in your eyes. What's her name if not Lady Jordan Skye? I remember how crazy you were about Princess Susanna's sister. Don't tell me it's still her after all these years."

"Avery?" Colin sputtered and growled. "Of course not." He peered across the dance floor toward the orchestra. Sarah dug in territory not open for inspection. "If you must know, your perfume is in my eyes." He made a face, leaning away from her, grinning, teasing. "If this is D'amond, we'll all be passed out before night's end."

"You're so full of lies, Prince Colin." She laughed, stepped into him, and rested her chin on his shoulder. "But you're very cute so I'll let you off the hook."

"Let me turn the tables. Who are you in love with, Sarah?"

"Guy Smoot, of course. But if you tell him I'll deny every word, then hunt you down in your sleep."

"Then you rather like the bickering Bickerson thing?"

"For now. Until he's ready."

The music changed and a shout rose from the crowd as the jaunty tune for the Farmer's Reel began. Men and women divided into sides and faced each other across the dance floor.

Colin bowed to Sarah as she curtseyed. Behind her, in the second row of reelers, Guy bowed to Jordan.

The violinist's bow bounced off the strings, raising the notes into a song.

Colin moved to the rhythm, dancing the familiar steps with precision, clasping hands, turning, spinning, reaching the end of the line, finding himself next to David, then turning to land face-to-face with Avery Truitt.

Her brown eyes met his on a level plane, and everything stopped. The music. The dance. His own heartbeat.

"Avery?" His voice caught, trapped in his dry throat.

"Hello, Colin." Her expression, confident and assured, reflected in his memories of her.

"Hello . . . Avery." Time had carved lean angles into her face, the roundness of her teen years gone. She was . . . stealing his breath.

The dancers moved around him. "Prince Colin, get a move on."

"See you." With a quick smile, Avery danced on, leaving behind the fragrance of southern seas. Of the shores of Georgia.

"Prince Colin, are you dancing or watching?" An older woman grabbed his hand, drawing him into the cross step and back around.

"Yes, of course, my apologies." He stumbled through the reel, his pulse racing when Avery crossed over to him and linked her hand with his, her touch a lightning bolt to his dull senses. *Say something, you daft man. Speak.* But he had no words. When she gazed at him, her expression sapped his strength.

"You're here," he managed, a weak mutter.

"And you're there," she said, the flash of her smile melting every bone in his body. Then she danced on.

When the reel ended, the dancers applauded one another and the orchestra. The ballroom was warm from the dance and the laughter. The footmen swung open the doors leading to the portico, letting in the brisk night air.

Couples moved to the refreshment tables and Colin stood alone. Jordan was always in such demand he typically saw her only when they arrived and when they left. At the moment, he was grateful since he needed to think.

What was Avery doing here? Well, of course, the Princess of Brighton was her sister. Why shouldn't she be here? Her mum was.

Colin tugged on his collar. 'Twas warm in here.

From the dais, Nathaniel addressed his guests, welcoming them, saying a prayer in a low and steady tone with a resonance Colin envied.

Nathaniel prayed with bold faith. As if he understood that the One he petitioned heard him. As though the Lord really cared.

Upon Nathaniel's "Amen," the orchestra started up with "God Bless the King and Country." Colin joined in the ancient song. Dad's rich bass rose beside him as he came alongside, handing Colin a glass, the bottom barely covered with a golden brown liquid.

"To the harvest." He raised his glass in toast. "And a lovely Christmas season."

"To the harvest and Christmas." Colin tapped his crystal glass with Dad's.

Dad took a short sip, then held the glass in his hands. "I see Avery Truitt is here."

"I just came across her myself." Colin stared at the floor, swirling the liquid in his glass. "She seems to be having a lovely time with Lord Chrysler."

"Are you holding steady? It's been too long to still harbor feelings for her, but I thought I'd ask."

"All is in hand, Dad." Colin reached for a nearby table, setting his glass aside. "No need to worry."

"As I thought." He motioned across the ballroom floor. "Your mum's talking with Lady Jordan. I've been thinking about a spring engagement with a fall wedding."

"For Jay and me?" Colin laughed, but Dad's somber expression stifled his merriment. "You're serious."

"I never joke about money or marriage."

Colin snapped his shoulders back, squaring up his resolve. "Dad, I'll propose to the woman I want when I want. You raised me to be my own man. Trust me in this matter. I'm your son." He popped his hand on his father's shoulder. "I come from good stock."

Dad nodded, tossing back the last of his drink. "Fine then. I'll leave you to sort it out. It's just . . . you're my shining star, Colin, what every father wants in a son, in an heir. When you walked in with Jordan tonight, your future unfurled before me. I realized what a power couple you could be. Perhaps it's time to move toward a more permanent arrangement." Dad set his glass down, taking a step back. "But I'll leave it to you. No more shop talk. As long as you know how proud I am of you."

Shop talk? Did Dad view marriage as a business deal? Alone with his thoughts, the beating of his heart in his ears, Colin considered Dad's proposal.

He never believed Lady Jordan was the one for him. He and Dad were not on the same page in this matter. And they might never be.

Colin had once believed Avery Truitt was the one for him. Until Dad showed him the "light."

However, with her perfume lingering in the ballroom air

somewhere, he began to wonder. Dad had misread Colin's relationship with Jordan. Could it be he'd misjudged Colin's relationship with Avery?

For the length of two reels and a waltz, Colin remained in the dance floor shadows, remembering Avery and nothing else.

CHAPTER 5

She escaped David after the last dance and tucked into a corner behind the food and drink displays, cradling a cup of cherry punch in her trembling hands, sorting through her feelings, dealing with the low fire burning under her skin.

He was . . . as amazing as she remembered. How could she manage to convince her heart otherwise? Prince Colin was the same ruddy and handsome man she'd fallen for five years ago.

One peek at him and she was seventeen again, waking up at three a.m. to check for his "Good morning, beautiful" text.

Sipping from her crystal cup, she tasted nothing but regret. Why did he leave her? What happened between them?

Should she just walk across the ballroom, tap him on the shoulder, and ask, "Tattersall, what gives?"

But he was with his friends and Lady Jordan, who was even more beautiful in person than in her photographs.

Worse, she couldn't tell if the rapid pace of her pulse was from true love or nervous energy over the man who rudely rejected her.

"Good evening, Avery."

She whirled around to the face of the elder Tattersall, Sir Edward, the captain of industry and Colin's father.

"Good evening." Avery lowered her punch, wishing to dismiss her cup. But she was several feet away from the table.

"Please, call me Edward. All of Colin's friends do." He leaned on the word *friend*, over-pronouncing the *d*, his accent sharp and pristine—like his smile, like his features.

"I wasn't sure you remembered me."

"I remember all of Colin's mates."

She had been more than a mate. Was he aware she loved his son? That he'd loved her?

Colin never divulged how much he shared with his father. Avery knew they were close but not the intimacies of their relationship.

"What brings you to our fair city?" The man's smile was practiced and perfect.

"My sister. The Christmas season." Avery stooped, setting her cup on the floor, along the wall, fearful she'd drop it. "Mama wanted the family to be together. My father died in the summer, you see."

"Yes, I'd heard. I'm so sorry for your loss."

"Thank you." What did this man want? Was he, too, sorry Colin dismissed her like a worn shoe?

"What do you think of my son and Lady Jordan Skye? Quite a stunning pair, are they not?" Sir Edward turned toward the dance floor as the next reel began.

Heat waved over Avery. Was this the reason he walked over? "Very handsome. Straight out of a fairy tale." The edge of her comment dragged with sarcasm. But if Edward heard it, he didn't acknowledge.

"Destined for great things, both of them. Have you seen her romantic comedy? Very well done. She has great comedic timing."

"A laugh a minute."

The man glared at her, then chuckled. "You Americans and your dry wit."

A man approached from another direction, his hair mussed, his bow tie swinging around his neck. "Edward, ole chap, you must hear this. Randall nearly killed himself skiing."

"Not again," he said. "I'll be along in a minute." He turned to Avery, his expression calculating if not a bit cold. "What were we saying? Oh yes, about Colin and Lady Jordan. Quite a power pair those two. Colin is set to take over the Tattersall fortune one day. We have parliament in our sights as well. Prince Colin could be the first royal elected to the governing body."

"Wouldn't that be something?" She didn't know what else to say.

"Indeed. I'm sure you, as the rest of his friends, will cheer him on."

"Of course." Avery gripped her hands at her waist. Where was he driving this conversation?

"Lady Jordan is a good match for a man of industry as well as politics, don't you think?"

"I don't know Lady Jordan at all, so I can't say."

"Forgive me, of course. How long has it been since you've seen Colin?"

"Four and a half years."

He jutted his chin in acknowledgement, then turned to go. "Enjoy your time in Brighton. I'm sure I'll see you at one of the family dinners. Good evening to you."

"Good evening." Avery faced the ballroom and the music,

quivering. The conversation with Sir Edward left her uneasy. As for Colin and his future . . . Good luck to him.

"Why the pensive expression?" a voice whispered in her ear. Colin peeked around. "You look rather glum, standing here alone. Prettiest girl in the room shouldn't be frowning."

"Prettiest?" Avery averted her gaze. "Did Lady Jordan leave already?"

Colin laughed. Didn't she love the music of his merriment. "I mean you."

Avery popped a grin. "I'm not frowning, see."

He held her gaze for a long moment. "It's good to see you."

"Y-you too." But she trembled under his laser allure. "Your father seems keen on you and Lady Jordan." Avery was tired of hidden things.

"My father spoke to you of me and Lady Jordan?"

"Yes, just now. He said you were destined for great things and Lady Jordan was perfect to go along for the ride."

Colin clapped his hands behind his back, gazing away from Avery, nodding toward someone across the room. "Dad likes to express his opinion."

"You don't agree?"

He regarded her. "Not necessarily."

Where did she go from here? Avery cut a glance over at him. At six foot plus with heels, she was level with him, face-to-face, eye-to-eye. When he caught her staring a warm blush spread through her.

"I should go." She skipped over to the table, setting down her cup.

But Colin caught her, his hand clapping hold of her arm. "Avery, wait."

She peeked at him, slipping free. "Wait for what?"

He swallowed, searching her eyes. "First of all, I'm sorry about your dad. I liked him a lot. He was a good man. Always kind to me."

"He was the best." Why was he doing this? The sting of tears rising behind her eyes threatened to embarrass her.

"And for what it's worth, I'm sorry about what happened between us." He sighed, pressing his hand against the back of his neck.

"It was a long time ago, Colin." She lost her jitters and found her nerve.

"Right. But I need to . . . well, I'm sorry how things ended."

"Did things end?" She made a face, mocking him and for the moment, not caring. "I simply recall a text saying you couldn't come over for prom and then—*poof*—nothing. Never heard from you again." She angled away from him, watching the dancers. The stinging tears fought their way back to the surface.

"I'm sorry, I should've talked to you. I was behind in school and Dad felt I was losing focus."

"So it was his idea for you to dump me? As if escorting me to a high school prom would've ruined your life?"

"He didn't want me to dump you . . . I didn't dump you . . . You have to think like him. Future, future, future. With him, even the way one brushes one's teeth impacts the future."

"You did dump me, Colin. Evidenced by the cone of silence."

"I didn't dump you."

"Whatever . . ."

Colin tugged at his collar, muttering to himself. "I'm sorry, but I had to consider my future. Dad made me see I needed to focus or fail."

"And that was impossible to tell me?"

Asking the questions relieved a tension she'd carried for a long time. A punching belief that he'd walked out of her life because she wasn't good enough.

"I admit, I didn't handle it well. I thought just cutting off communication would make it easier for both of us."

"It wasn't easy for me." She crossed her arms, holding herself together.

He sighed. But when he looked at her square on, compassion molded his expression. "My father discovered how much I'd spent flying to see you. He called the university for my grades, and they weren't good. He feared for my future."

"Did you tell him I was on you about your studies? That I questioned the money you spent flying to see me?"

"Didn't matter to him. It was proof of my wrong focus. He asked me not to see you again."

With the lovely music and dance flowing around them, Avery learned the ugly truth.

Avery relaxed her stance. "Why didn't you tell me?"

He shrugged, the countenance of a confident prince fading to rebuked son. "Didn't know how to tell you."

"How about the truth? Did you want us to end? Was your dad the catalyst?"

Colin mulled on her question. "I'm not sure."

She sighed. Well, now she knew. The gnawing she wrestled with whenever Colin came to mind must cease.

"There you are, darling." Lady Jordan emerged from the crowd. "I lost you." She peered up at Avery. "Goodness, I thought I was seeing things when I glanced over here, but you really are quite tall."

"Jordan," Colin said. "This is—"

"The Princess of Brighton's sister. I know. I saw you on the dais earlier."

"Avery Truitt," she said, offering her hand.

"Jordan Skye."

"Nice to meet you. I enjoyed your last movie."

"Really? How splendid. Good to hear from an American. I've not visited the States enough." She turned to Colin, intimately touching his shoulder. "Darling, please, can we sit?" She pointed to a plush purple velvet settee. "My feet are killing me. These shoes looked great in the magazines but . . ." She made a face and moved to the settee. "Avery, I hear you play volleyball."

"I did. In college."

"I played lacrosse. Made All-League at uni." Jordan sat down with a glance at Colin, patting the spot next to her.

Of course she did. She had it all. No wonder Sir Edward liked her.

"So how do you two know each other?" Jordan said.

Avery peered at Colin. *Do you want to tell this story?*

"We met a few years back," he said, easing down on the settee next to Jordan. "At Nathaniel's coronation."

"Oh marvelous. Why didn't you tell me you knew the princess's sister?" She leaned against him with a glance at Avery. "He's full of secrets, this one."

"That's rather overstating," Colin said, flustered. "I don't have secrets."

"Darling, everyone has secrets." Jordan smiled. "Even Avery here, right?"

"Not really." She felt raw and transparent. Could they see the truth in her eyes? The flutter of her dress where her heart pounded?

"Avery, what do you love about Brighton? Oh, Colin, I forgot to tell you, Jeremiah Gonda is considering a movie based on the Pembroke Chapel lore. He likes me for the part of Lady Charlene." Jordan's chortle embodied her. Alluring and sexy. Avery was a wilting flower in comparison. "Success is not what you know but who you know. Anyway, Madeline and Hyacinth got everyone thinking about the old bell-ringing tradition. Have you heard of it, Avery? A young man smitten with love runs up to the Pembroke bell tower and pulls the bell cord just after midnight of the Harvest Celebration, chiming his love for all to hear."

"I've not heard of it, no."

Jordan patted the settee again. "Sit, please. I'll have a kink in my neck looking up at you."

Colin scooted over for Avery to sit next to him. Why oh why couldn't she just excuse herself? This conversation was like watching a train wreck. She couldn't quite escape the fascination of it all, sitting here with Colin, with Lady Jordan, questions rising in her mind now that she'd heard the truth from Colin.

She understood the pressure from his father. Even understood why he had to back out of prom. But the silence, cutting her off without a word? They used to talk about everything. So why not that?

". . . isn't that crazy, Avery? The chap who rings the bell must win his true love's heart and marry her by Christmas." Jordan chatted on about this bell tower tradition. "I spoke with Hyacinth and she's just dying for someone to ring the bell this year." She dropped her arm over Colin's leg. "What do you think, darling? Is anyone smitten enough in this room to ring the bell?"

"Not just in this room but any man across the city." He adjusted his position, appearing uncomfortable, avoiding a direct look at

Avery. So it seemed to her. "The country, for that matter. If he's determined. If he can get here in time."

"A minute past midnight," Jordan said with a toss of her hair. "We shall see. What do you think, Avery? Would you marry someone who tried to woo you in twenty-four days?"

"Depends on who it was."

"Say, David there." She waved at Lord Chrysler as he passed. "Or Prince Colin here."

Avery swallowed, an unbidden heat creeping across her cheeks. "I-I don't know. What about you? Would you marry someone, say Prince Colin, in twenty-four days if he rang the bell for you?"

Colin shifted forward, glancing askance at Avery, his brow furrowed.

"Colin, would you ring the bell for me?" Jordan's posture was a blend of teasing and beckoning. "How romantic."

"Yeah, well, no one is ringing the bell tonight. Especially me."

"Especially you?" Jordan laughed, not offended, so assured and self-aware. "And why is that?"

"I don't believe in true love."

"What? Darling, you're joking. Who doesn't believe in true love?" Jordan demanded in a lilting tone. "If I didn't believe in true love, I'm not sure I could breathe. What about you, Avery?"

"Nope, I don't believe in true love either."

"Neither one of you? Tsk, tsk, we must do something about this. Avery, after what happened to your sister, surely you believe in fairy tales. Don't you want to find your own prince one day?"

"Maybe at one time I did." Avery stood to go. "But not anymore."

CHAPTER 6

11:50 p.m.

Kicking the brush aside, Colin ran the wooded shadows of the barrier forest surrounding Stratton Palace. He'd left the dance with Guy, grabbing the rucksacks the man had stuffed beneath the palace hedge, and escaped in the high moonlight, the horizon edged in the amber and white glow of city lights.

Situated in the middle of Cathedral City, Stratton Palace sat on the tip of three hundred acres of wooded land. An oasis amid the busyness and hubbub of capital city life.

An arm of the River Condor ran along the eastern border, and Colin spent a good many summer afternoons of his youth fishing from those waters.

But tonight was about his private tradition. And escaping Avery. Since their conversation, he'd been bothered. Unsettled.

"Watch out for that limb." Guy ducked as he ran, laughing, his rucksack slipping from his shoulder.

During the week Guy was a driven entrepreneur, launching Internet businesses, selling space and services. But tonight he and Colin were kids again, carefree, climbing to the top of the tower with their pints and pipes, waxing the new day and Christmas season with sentimental conversations about their youth.

The pint bottles clicked in his rucksack as Colin dodged the low swung limb, breaking into the opening, sprinting the short distance to the edge of the woods to the Pembroke tower door.

Colin butted up to the rough-hewn boards, drawing a deep breath, laughing. "You know, we're not fifteen anymore. We don't have to escape the ballroom like errant boys. We can just walk across the lawn if we want."

"Where's the fun in that? Besides, if anyone sees us, it's a footrace for the press." Guy motioned for Colin to open the door. "Come on. It's cold."

Colin dropped his rucksack to the stone step and produced his lock-picking tools and a torch. He'd tried to get the key proper a few years ago, but Nathaniel didn't see any need for keys to the dangerous old family chapel to be floating about the city.

Then he wanted to know why Colin wanted a key. Did he intend to go into the cold tower with its slick, dangerous steps? In fact, Nathaniel wanted to investigate the place and maybe tear it down. So Colin shut up afterward, content to pick the lock.

"What's taking so long?" Guy said.

"Don't rush me. The old padlock gets rustier year by year."

"Do you think some lovesick chap saw the Madeline and Hyacinth show? Come round wanting to ring the bell?"

"Look around, mate. We're the only ones here. And if one does break for it, we'll be there to stop him, talk some sense into him."

Guy checked the time in the glow of his torch light. "Eleven fifty-five. We're running out of time."

The lock tumblers gave way and the padlock popped. Colin swung the door open with a step back and a bow. "You first. Age before beauty."

Guy wove his torch glow over the spiral, curved stairs. "One hundred and eighty-two slick, rounded steps. Let's go gently, mate, we don't want to Prince Michael—it to the tower floor."

Guy was the one who started this private tradition, dreaming up a moment to welcome the Christmas season with a lit tobacco pipe and hoisted pint. And for eight years, they'd kept it strong.

Colin burst through the door at the top of the tower, stumbling forward as the twelfth chime faded from the midnight air. Falling against the wall, he drew a deep breath, filled his lungs, then leaned out the nearest open, stone arch.

"To the Christmas season." He yanked his pipe and pint from his sack.

Guy joined him, his bottle raised. "To Christmas."

"And a happy holiday."

"To love."

"To love?" Colin made a face at his friend, downing a swallow of the bitter brew. It was an old Brightonian drink developed by the miners to sustain them in the long hot afternoons.

"To love. Isn't that what this tower represents? First love to God, if you're into that sort of thing. Then to the woman of your heart." Guy raised his bottle to the moon. "To love."

"You sound as if you want to ring the bell, Guy. To win Lady Sarah by Christmas Day."

"I can't believe my ears. Reverse your words. Do you want

me in an early grave?" Guy leaned against the arch posts. "Now, you . . . you have two great choices."

"The bitters are talking, man. I have no choices."

"Are you blind? You have Lady Jay. She's gorgeous. And that giant girl. Avery. Wow. You never said she had pins like that. Up to her neck."

"Stop, Guy. Just stop talking."

"Ah, I've touched on something. What is it? Are you thinking of ringing the bell? The first after 182 years? It's only fitting it should be a prince." Guy nudged him with his bottle. "Come on, man, break the curse of Prince Michael."

"I'm not ringing the bell." Colin glanced up at the ancient thing. "I doubt it will even ring anymore."

"Then what's the harm? Give the rope a tug. Come on, tell me, who would you ring the bell for, Colin? Isn't that part of our tradition? To bare our souls?"

"If you're so keen, you tell me. Who would you ring the bell for?"

Guy swigged at his drink, grinning. "Sarah."

"Sarah? Ha! Really? For all your guff, you're in love with her?"

"Shhh, keep your voice down. With her big bat ears, she's bound to hear you."

"This is huge news, mate. Why not tell her?"

"And ruin all the fun?" Guy angled through the archway. "Besides, what if she turns me down?"

"Coward." Should he break the news? Sarah loved him. Or leave him to figure it out for himself?

"Ha, I don't see you ringing the bell for the woman you love."

"Because I don't love anyone."

"Liar."

"Better than being a coward."

"At least I admitted I love her. I just haven't told her yet. You can't even admit that much."

Colin sobered. "There's nothing to admit."

The friends fell silent. Then Guy raised his pint to the moon once more. "To love, with all its mysteries."

Colin hoisted his bottle as well but didn't salute love. Not when Avery was so close but yet so far. How easy it had been to clear the air and tell the truth. Well, most of it. The rest she'd never know. What good would it do?

"What is it about love that's so terrifying, Colin?"

He leaned farther through the arch, looking around at Guy, whose typically perfect hair whispered over his forehead in the slight breeze.

"People make it hard. I don't suppose that was ever the good Lord's intention."

The city spreading before them, just beyond the trees, was one of Colin's favorite views. Next to him, Guy remained quiet, contemplative.

Turning the other way, Colin dealt with the burden of his heart. Seeing Avery brought it all back. She fascinated him. He liked her. No, he loved her.

"Lord," he spoke under his breath, over the opening of his pint, "I'd ring the bell for Avery if she could be my wife."

Colin closed his eyes, imagining his words winging before the throne of heaven where the immortal, invisible, wise God who watched over the universe also watched over him.

The breeze stilled. Then . . .

A clattering raised behind him. Colin turned just as the bell began to swing, the heavy bronze piece sweeping from side to side, higher and higher as if rising from a deep sleep. Chills skirted over his skin.

Colin whipped around to his friend. Was he holding the bell cord? "Guy, what in the world, chap?"

But he was pressed against the wall, hands over his ears. The bell rang higher, clanging louder and louder.

Colin crossed to the pull cord. The weathered and frayed hemp remained hooked to the wall. The ringing vibrated through him, stealing his breath, stealing his thoughts.

"Let's get out of here." Guy snatched his rucksack and made for the stairs.

"I'm behind you." Collecting his gear, Colin dashed for the steps, his foot slipping over the stone. Tumbling forward, he caught himself on the rickety railing, his bottle of bitters sailing from his hand, spinning down, down, down and crashing on the tower floor.

Guy shined the light on his face. "That was close."

From the tower, the bell rang, raising its chime higher and higher.

"What is going on with that blasted bell?"

Colin knew. Sure as St. Nick was Father Christmas, he knew. *God, what are You doing?* "Just go. Before everyone in the palace hears and meets us at the tower door."

"I've got the willies," Guy muttered. "The tower is haunted. Prince Michael is ringing the bell from beyond the grave."

"Don't be silly, mate." Colin urged Guy down the slick steps. He didn't know about ghosts or Prince Michael hauntings, but he understood when God answered a prayer.

But what did it mean?

When they arrived at the bottom, Guy stopped, pressing his hand into Colin's chest. "I'll go out first. Otherwise, it's curtains for you. Everyone will think you rang the bell and the press will be mad about you marrying Lady Jay."

"What about you? Won't they expect something of you?"

"Only that I'd pull such a prank. I'm not a prince so I'll take the heat, be the first one out. You run on my flank and sneak around to the other side of the tower. Return to the palace when all the brouhaha has died down."

Colin clapped his friend on the shoulder. "I'll owe you one."

"Think nothing of it. How can I let a prince in Brighton be accused of ringing the harvest bell for the first time in nearly two hundred years? It'd be madness." Guy started to go out, then paused. "But mate to mate, in the name of tradition, when that bell rang, for whatever crazy reason, you were thinking of someone, weren't you? Tell ole Guy. Come on."

Colin shook his head. "Listen, I hear voices. They're coming."

Guy hunkered down. "Ready?"

Colin squatted down on Guy's right side. If memory served, there was a dip in the lawn just beyond the tower. He would hit the ground rolling and hide in the shadows.

"Ready? Go!" Guy kicked open the door, but instead of running out, he pressed against the opposite tower wall. Colin, however, already in motion, dashed into the blinding flash of cameras.

"Prince Colin, you rang the bell!"

"For whom did the bell toll?"

"Do you intend to marry her on Christmas Day?"

"Did you ring it for Lady Jordan? Hey! Is she out here? Lady Jay, what do you say?"

"No, no, please . . ." He held up his hands, shielding his eyes from the blinding lights. Guy, that rotten, no good . . . The lad had done some contemptible things in their long friendship, but this took the cake. "I didn't ring the bell."

The gathering of reporters and onlookers laughed. "Right, then who did?"

God? He'd be a laughingstock. "Guy Smoot." Colin pointed to the tower. "He was with me. Why don't you ask him?"

"Come on, Prince Colin. Tell us. There's no Guy Smoot is there?"

Colin peeked into the tower. Guy was not to be found. He'd escaped on the flank and rolled away into the shadows.

Facing the press, Colin gathered his courage. "There's nothing to say. I'm telling the truth. I did not ring the chapel bell."

CHAPTER 7

The entire ballroom pressed through the open doors onto the portico at midnight when the city's cathedral bells rang—a glorious, haunting sound.

Six exquisite stone and marble structures set at different points in the city chimed the midnight hour in unison, and the palace was smack-dab in the middle of them all. The vibration shook Avery so she couldn't feel her own heartbeat.

The cold air felt good against her warm skin. She'd learned two new reels, thanks to David, and spent the last half hour stepping, tapping, making figure eights, spinning around, crossing from side to side . . . and laughing. She needed to laugh. To finally close and lock the door marked Prince Colin.

It was good to hear the truth. No matter how painful. But his rejection lingered with her longer than she liked.

When the twelfth chime rang out, its low peeling gong reverberating from what seemed like every direction, Nathaniel called to the guests.

"Welcome the Christmas season. May it be happy for each one of you!"

The guests on the portico cheered in salute, wishing the king and all his family the very same, turning back inside the ballroom where they would dance until dawn.

Avery leaned against the stone railing, raising her face to the wind, relishing the last glorious round of the cathedral chimes. Like a round robin. She imagined heaven must sound somewhat like those bells.

Then, as if late to the ball, a lone bell rang out. Its rich bass tone was not robust like the cathedral bells, but rich and haunting, declaring a message all its own.

The guests paused, listening, their voices starting low, then rising in an excited buzz.

"Pembroke?"

"The chapel bell . . ."

"Is someone in the bell tower?"

"What's this? Some chap declaring his love?"

A photographer shoved past Avery and down the steps, yelling, "By King Stephen, someone rang the bell!"

Three more photographers followed, the glow of their flashlights weaving and bobbing over the ground. The lovely and bejeweled TV chick, Hyacinth, took off like a shot with her cameraman.

"I knew it, I knew it!"

Avery pushed forward to the edge of the marble porch, leaning toward the sound, her heart fluttering in her chest, the tone of that particular bell not echoing through her but settling in and sinking down. For a moment she couldn't breathe.

David came alongside her. "Don't tell me some poor fool rang the old chapel bell." He chuckled, glancing over at her. "They're bringing out the hot cider. Do you care for a cup?"

"Why would he be a fool?"

Some of the guests were into it now, scrambling off the portico, using their phones as lights, running into the palace shadows toward the sound of the bell, still ringing, loud and clear.

"To win his true love by Christmas. Not an easy feat. Ah, there's Guy Smoot. My good man, who rang the bell?"

Guy made his way over, hands in his pockets. "No telling, though I hear it might have been Prince Colin."

Colin? Avery fell against the cold stone. *Do not tell me I am here to witness it firsthand.*

The head butler appeared in the wide doorway, a dark silhouette against the bright lights of the ballroom. "Hot cider, tea, and cocoa everyone. And in His Majesty's honor, baskets of puffs."

Puffs. Nathaniel's favorite. A light but chewy Brighton donut dipped in brown sugar and cinnamon.

"Shall we?" David offered his arm.

Avery hesitated, staring out over the grounds, her heart searching for Colin. He'd seemed so dead set against ringing the bell earlier. Was it all a ruse?

"Who are you looking for?" David whispered in her ear.

"No one." Avery glanced up at him. "Just curious about all the hubbub."

"Believe me, we'll know the story soon enough." David led her inside, toward the refreshment tables. "Madeline and Hyacinth will be all over this. Whoever rang the bell . . . his life will not be his own."

"His? What if it was a she?" Avery imagined Lady Jordan capable of such a thing.

"A she? Well, that'd be a twist in the tale. I like your thinking, Miss Avery. Ah, here we are. The famous puffs."

As David handed her a china plate painted with holly leaves, a commotion on the dance floor drew her eye.

Colin, surrounded by reporters, photographers, and the TV presenter Hyacinth, strode through the ballroom with dark intent.

". . . but no one has rung the bell in 182 years." Hyacinth skipped alongside the prince, trying to keep up, her tight skirt hindering her stride.

"I'm well aware of the years that have passed, but I tell you, I did not ring the bell." Colin kept walking with purpose but without aim, shooting Avery a side glance as he passed, his eyes reflecting the frustration in his voice.

The orchestra was in place again, picking up their instruments, filling the ballroom with the first Christmas song of the season.

The dancers and watchers gathered around the bandstand, their voices raised in song.

"Oh come all ye faithful, joyful and triumphant . . ."

Avery sang, scanning the perimeter, finding Colin tucked in the shadows of the columns in an intimate face-to-face with Lady Jordan. She tried not to stare, but couldn't quite glance away.

They appeared to be arguing. Lady Jordan walked off, then spun back around to him, arms flailing.

This was not a pleasant night, rather morning, for him.

The orchestra played another carol, a haunting, mournful sound. "O Come, O Come Emmanuel."

Tears slicked over Avery's eyes, the minor notes raising her sentiments, missing Daddy, missing what she'd dreamed of with Colin. The five months she loved him sowed deep hope into her heart.

The last night she'd been with him, they stayed up watching the Avenger movies series in the palace media room, eating two boxes of puffs they'd found in the palace kitchen, debating the plot and story line of the characters, what was real and what was not—none of it—then fighting over which superhero best fit them.

Colin wanted Ironman, but Avery had her eye on the suit long before she met Colin. He tried to squeeze her into being Natasha.

"Why, because I'm a girl? I think you'd make a great Natasha."

"You're out of your ever loving mind. I'd be Loki before Natasha."

"Loki? Perfect!" She laughed hard. "You to a T."

"You can't be serious. Take that back."

He'd grabbed her and pulled her to him, leaning back against the sofa cushions, kissing her, his lips so sweet, so very, very sweet.

In the morning, there was chaos in the royal kitchen. Where were the puffs? They had been ordered for Nathaniel's breakfast with the prime minister and parliament leaders.

Oops . . .

She and Colin never laughed so hard, hopping into his car, racing to Franklin's Bakery at five a.m., banging on the back door, begging Mr. Franklin to open for emergency puffs.

"Avery?" David leaned to see her face. "You're smiling. What's funny?"

"Just remembering something."

"Care to share?" David's flirting fell on fallow ground. Colin had spoiled her for any other man. A truth she must get over. "Oh, look, there's Colin with Jordan. I think we can assume the prince did ring the bell. For her."

"You think he did?" She tried to sound casual, nonchalant. "What would you do, David? Would you ring the bell for Lady Jordan? She's gorgeous and sexy, famous, wealthy, seems rather down to earth." Ah, Colin must have rung the bell for her. She was perfect for him and his aristocratic, parliamentary future.

David angled close, lacing his fingers with Avery's, the intimate move catching her unaware. "Lady Jay is not really my type." He tossed her a wink that both warmed and disturbed her. "I rather like my women tall with auburn hair and a Southern accent."

CHAPTER 8

December 1
Twenty-four days until Christmas

Madeline & Hyacinth Live! Show

Madeline: "We have a great show for you
    all today. We are so excited."
Hyacinth: "Beyond excited, love."
Madeline: "Hy was at the palace last night
    when Prince Colin *actually* rang the
    old Pembroke Chapel bell—"
Hyacinth: "But hold on, Maddie. The
    prince denies ringing the bell."
Madeline: "Yet he was the only one at the bell tower."
Hyacinth: "Exactly! So there's a mystery.
    Why is he denying it? Did he change

his mind on the way down? Who did he
ring the bell for in the first place?"

Madeline: "All things we are going to discuss on today's
show. (She swept her hand toward the screen
behind her.) And we are counting down to the
revelation of for 'whom the bell tolled' from now
until Christmas Eve." (The audience applauded.)

Hyacinth: "We have exclusive footage. The bell
ringing has sparked a new fascination for
the old tradition. Twitter is going crazy
over 'Who *really* rang the bell?'"

Madeline: "But you were there, Hy. You saw
the prince come *out* of the bell tower."

Hyacinth: "Indeed, which we will show to our
viewers in a minute." She pointed to a bell
tally behind her on the set. "We want you all
to keep track with us. Our staff worked all
weekend to create an app for you to download.
Did Prince Colin ring the bell? If so, for whom?
Share with friends, make new friends, enter
your guesses until midnight Christmas Eve.
We'll pull a winner the day after Christmas."

Madeline: "Who will get to spend New Year's Eve
with us on the first ever televised New Year's
show." (The audience cheered and applauded.)

Hyacinth: "I so want a royal Christmas wedding."
She sighed. "Prince Colin swears he did *not* ring
the bell. But I'm sure he's trying to throw us off.
I saw him come out of the bell tower while the
bell still chimed. If he didn't ring it, who did?"

Madeline: "Viewers, if you see or hear anything
suspicious, call the show or pop a message
on our Facebook page. Or tweet your
discovery to @madandhyliveshow with
the hashtag #princecolinrangthebell."

December 3
Twenty-two days until Christmas

Colin didn't bother to look at the morning headlines. Both the *Liberty Press* and the *Informant* were still running stories about the history of the bell ringing and printing pictures of Colin coming out of the tower, speculating when he would officially propose to Lady Jordan.

This was not how he planned to start the Christmas season. The joyful sounds of the Christmas melodies playing from the speakers in his office failed to reach the sentimental parts of his soul. Instead, he was agitated and on edge. It seemed the season was ruined before it started.

From Colin's office door, Dad knocked. "Did you see the papers? They are still going on about you."

"I've stopped reading them." He tipped the folded newsprint into the trash bin by his desk. "Did Hornsby get hold of you? He says there's trouble brewing with the union in Hessenberg. We won't meet the production quotas if things don't get ironed out."

"I'm on a conference call at ten. I'd like you to sit in." Dad eased down into a chair across from Colin. "Well? Do you want to talk about this business with the bell?"

Colin looked up from his phone. "I can make the ten o'clock call." Being on a team charged with new business development, he spent a lot of his time researching and meeting with entrepreneurs across Western Europe. "And what's to talk about? The bell rang when I just happened to be in the tower."

Dad chuckled, sitting back, crossing his legs. "The papers say you accidentally rang the bell. How does one *accidentally* ring a six-hundred-pound chapel bell? Did you trip? Fall over the railing and reach for the bell cord to save your life?"

"I never said it was an accident. I'm saying I didn't ring it at all." Colin paced to the window, his twentieth-floor office providing an ethereal view of Cathedral City and the river winding along the eastern perimeter. "They assumed it was an accident."

"Then who rang the bell?"

Colin looked back at his father. A driven man, Sir Edward Tattersall had no use for faith in his robust life.

Colin had a lot in common with his dad—sports, love of the outdoors, the navy, the family business—but when he encountered the living Lord the summer he turned sixteen while on a camping expedition with his church group, his path diverged from his father's.

A mutual faith was one of the reasons he loved Avery. She shared his love for all things holy.

"Colin? Did you hear me? Who rang the bell?"

"You wouldn't believe me if I told you."

"Try me."

A knock echoed on Colin's door. Dad's assistant, Eden, slipped in with a cup of coffee. He thanked her and took a long sip, eyeing Colin over the rim.

"What does it matter, Dad? I'm not marrying anyone on Christmas Day."

Dad lowered his cup, resting it on the saucer. "Were you alone that night?"

"Smoot was with me."

Dad narrowed his gaze. "Did he ring the bell?"

"No." As much as he'd like to put this off on Guy—and wouldn't it be his just deserts?—he refused to settle the score in public. Those moves tended to get messy and ruin relationships. He'd square with Guy another way. Make no mistake.

"Then it had to be you, son. Why are you trying to dodge the matter? Has Lady Jordan agreed to marrying on Christmas Day? Best get on with it. Women like Lady Jay need time to prepare a gown. Every designer in the Western world will vie for her business." Once Dad took hold of a notion, there was no use trying to get him off it. "It's been so long since any man rang the Pembroke bell, your doing so makes it noteworthy. You're redeeming the curse of Prince Michael, bringing the tradition back to life." Dad's grin indicated his pleasure. "For centuries to come Brightonians will remember Prince Colin Edward Stratton Tattersall for launching the Harvest Celebration tradition again. After 182 years a brave man finally attempted the 182 steps to declare his love. That's sound bite material there. Good on you, son."

Colin leaned against the wall. He should just say it. But . . . "Sound bite material aside, I did not ring that bell. Do you want history to mark me for an achievement not my own?"

Dad leaned forward, his intense gaze drilling through Colin. "What's with all the hesitation? Why the fuss? Just admit you . . . Ah, I see. Jordan turned you down?"

Dad, the second son of a business magnet and entrepreneur, bore in his bones a desire to leave his mark in the world with his three children, with his massive business holdings, and by working the Tattersall name into royal and Brightonian history.

Marrying the daughter of his king was a grand start. Dad was also a traditionalist, a family man, wrapped up in Brightonian sentiment.

"She'd turn me down, no doubt. But I didn't ask her to marry me. Nor do I intend to do so." She was hopping mad that night. Wild in her protest that she'd not be manipulated into marriage when her career was at the tipping point.

"How dare you pull such a stunt, pressuring me into marriage. Everyone will be expecting . . ."

"Pardon me, but do you hear me proposing? Off your high horse, Jay. I've no intentions toward marriage."

The row continued, inspiring a spectacular headache.

"Colin, you're not making sense."

Of course not. Did the hand of God ever make sense to the unseeing? And oftentimes, even to the seeing?

"Smoot and I go to the tower every year," Colin began, leading Dad away from "Who rang the bell?" He didn't want to expose his heart, his prayer about Avery. The notion felt private. His alone to work out with his Lord. "At midnight. We take up a pint of bitters and a pipe, talk about the past . . . the future."

Dad's countenance darkened. "What are you not saying, Colin?"

"That our private tradition is now exposed. We'll probably never get back there alone. We'll have to fight the masses."

"Is this about the Truitt girl?"

"No . . . no." To his own ears, the response sounded like a lie.

But Dad didn't press. "I see. You don't want to come abreast with me." He stood, clattering his coffee cup against the saucer, checking his watch. "Nevertheless, I encourage you to make a go with Lady Jordan." Dad's smile, his personal seal of approval that Colin treasured, felt manipulative today. "She's perfect for you."

Said without question. Without a crack for Colin to object. His love for his father was frustrated only by the continued control the man longed to exercise in Colin's life.

Dad wasn't thinking. Because if he really wanted a solid match for his son, he'd see Lady Jordan was not the one. She had her own dreams and plans.

Colin's relationship with her was very different from the one he'd had with Avery. When he met Avery, he fell instantly in love. If a twenty-one-year-old university man could make such a claim.

Just thinking of her made his palms clammy and his heart pound. Sleep meant nothing to him if he could extend a FaceTime session with her.

More times than he could count, he woke up in the middle of the night, reached for his phone, and sent her a text. Thinking of you.

He ached, he missed her so much. What he thought would be a fun friendship turned into head-over-heels love. How could he settle for less?

His heart did not ache for Jordan. Or pine. He went days without thinking of her. When he woke in the night, he fluffed his pillow and drifted off to sleep again.

Colin returned to his desk, gathering his emotions, sorting through his diary.

"Colin, listen." Dad popped back in, his brow furrowed with advice. "Don't overthink this marriage business. It's an arrangement, a contract. You negotiate. Compromise. Make it work for all involved."

Colin regarded his father, refusing to be one with his cold and calculating suggestion. "I thought marriage was a covenant. You got my back, I got yours, we're in this together for the long haul. That love was the bond that held you together along with the commitment. I can't marry Jordan just because it's good business."

"Marriage is an arrangement. Sometimes from the heart. Sometimes the head. At best, a blend of both. Jordan is good for you, for us, our business, your future political career." Dad's eyes filling with the lightning of his argument. "It tells the kingdom you're a royal putting our nation first. You won't step aside to marry an American. What does it say to our women that our king and his brother married foreigners?"

"I hope it tells them to marry whom they love." Colin spied his cup of tea. He reached for a sip but the liquid had grown cold. "Is that why you married Mum, Dad? For advantage?"

"There was love involved. Affection. But it was also a good match. For both of us."

Colin sat back, his gaze fixed on the wall. "I'm going to let this thing die down. Lay low. Hopefully enjoy my Christmas." He'd wanted to go Christmas shopping this week, but with the press hounding him . . .

Dad surrendered his hands as he made his way to the door. "You're making too much of it. Just propose to Jordan, I highly doubt she'd turn you down. No matter what she said at the Harvest Celebration. By the way, your grandmother's ring is still in the vault at Lord & Gladwell." Dad paused at the door. "But I suppose you already know that, don't you?"

"Yes, I suppose I do."

CHAPTER 9

December 5
Twenty days until Christmas

Monday afternoon Avery met her sister in the palace garage, where two protection officers waited by a dark Range Rover.

She was on sister duty today, attending a Christmas fund-raiser with Susanna.

"Please come with me. It'll be fun. If you don't, I feel like we won't get much time together. My diary is so full . . ."

But she didn't have to ask twice, or pretend to beg. Avery loved being with her sister.

"Are we ready?" Susanna hurried across the garage, her heels clacking against the tiled floor.

The protection officer opened the back door for her to slip inside. Avery followed.

She'd awoken early to snow falling beyond the window, covering the palace grounds in white, the lights on the fir trees still glowing.

Avery pressed her head against the glass, thinking of Colin, the truth still stinging in her heart. She'd been a distraction. Someone to be dismissed for the sake of the big picture.

But she was for him. Wanted him to do all the things his father wanted him to do. She was on his case all the time about his studies and time management.

In her young life, she'd never dreamed of romance and marriage, but of playing volleyball and coaching. Even as a kid she loved to tutor her friends in whatever games they played.

Then she met Colin, and—*poof!*—Her desires vanished and a new longing settled in. At seventeen, Plan A became Plan B.

If she didn't marry Colin, then she'd play volleyball or coach. But she was crazy in love without a smidgen of doubt.

"You okay?" Susanna said.

Avery popped a smile for her sister. "I'm good." She tapped the window with her knuckle. "Loving the snow and all the Christmas decorations."

Brighton turned into an old world Christmas scene with costumed carolers and decorated homes and shops during this season.

"The snow will be interesting for the fund-raiser since it's outdoors in the park. We usually don't get this much snow in December."

"Yeah, so what is this thing we're going to?"

"Earn-A-Pound-Buy-A-Gift." Susanna smoothed her coat. "About a hundred children participated in a program that taught them how to make crafts to sell. Their earnings will go toward Christmas gifts they want to buy for family and friends."

"That should be fun. Even in the snow."

"It's quite lovely, really, set up like Santa's workshop. Lots of lights. Vendors selling hot chocolate and treats. Gas heaters along the thoroughfare. Last year was good fun."

"I'll look for something to buy my new niece or nephew."

"Avery . . ." Susanna's tone sobered. "Colin will be there."

She regarded Susanna, then shrugged. "It's a free country."

"We are co-patrons of this event."

"Good for him. And you." Avery stared out the window, watching modern Cathedral City pass by.

"Stop," Susanna said.

Avery glanced around. "Stop what?"

"All this pretending you don't care about him. I saw your face when he came back through the ballroom after he rang the bell. *If he rang the bell.* Who can believe what the papers say?"

"How could you see my face? You were across the room."

"I have X-ray eyes. Besides, I'm your sister and I know your posture from a thousand paces."

Avery laughed. "You'll always be the boss of me, won't you?"

"Yes." Then, "Do you still love him?"

"You already asked me that."

"I'm asking you again."

"No, I don't. And please don't ask me anymore."

As the car made its way through the narrow streets, under Christmas lights shining from post to post, the clouds broke and the sun painted the horizon a brilliant pink.

Avery leaned against her door, watching the old city go by, memories of her first trip to Cathedral City blending with her present reality. She'd hung out the window that day, so eager to see, to touch, to taste everything. She was so wide-eyed and open-hearted. Prime for Colin to walk in and take up residence.

"He didn't come to prom because his father said I was a distraction."

Susanna was silent until Avery peered at her. "I wondered. Edward's very exacting. Very ambitious for Colin."

"Don't blame him. I'd want the best for my kid too."

"What if the best for him is you?"

"Apparently I'm not."

"You don't know that for certain."

"Um, yeah, I think four and half years of silence is proof enough." The round-robin speculation knotted her insides.

"I just want you to be happy." Susanna squeezed Avery's hand. "I remember when you came along. Mama and Daddy had just gotten remarried. I was so excited. My family was healed. Then when they told me Mama was pregnant, I was so jealous. That baby would have the parents I didn't have. Then I held you in my arms for the first time and melted. You have that way about you, Avery. You melt hearts."

"Then again, nothing gets a twelve-year-old girl's heart like a sweet, soft baby."

"No, I'd held plenty of babies. It was you, your sweet . . . everything. Suddenly I couldn't remember life without you."

"What makes you tell that story?" Avery said.

"Daddy always said you were the seal on our family. Proof of God's love and miracles. And he spoiled you. We all did."

"What are you driving at, Suz?"

"Some things in life don't work out. So you loved Colin and he stupidly let you go. Sorry, I'm talking about it again. But none of this changes who you are, who God's called you to be. You are an amazing woman. Don't lose sight of who you are because a man can't appreciate you. Who cares what Colin wants? What his father wants? God is for you. What do you want out of life, Aves?"

"In the near future, to get a coaching job."

"Then go for it. You'll be a great coach. Now, what do you want for Christmas?" Susanna grinned. "I haven't started shopping yet."

They talked shopping and gift ideas, Christmases of the past, laughing, noting the Market Avenue shoppers, and the one man so burdened with bags they couldn't see his face.

"Two words for him: online shopping," Avery said, drawing a giggle from Suz.

But deep down, she was restless. Anxious about seeing Colin in a few minutes. Under her coat she was both hot and cold.

The truth was, she didn't know what she wanted except to be rid of her feelings for him. No matter what she told herself, they remained. She had to destroy them, somehow, and get over him. Once and for all.

The car pulled along the curb at Maritime Park-turned-winter-wonderland. The snowfall thickened as if on cue and the lush fir trees were trimmed with strings of colored lights.

The officers hopped out, opening Susanna's and Avery's doors.

Photographers hovered close, snapping pictures before security shoved them away. Along the crisscrossing walkways were the children, gathering at their booths with classmates, parents, and teachers, each booth decorated with their drawings of Christmas, the air thick with their excitement and laughter.

From the Strand amphitheater, a quintet played Christmas carols.

"Your Majesty, there you are." A stout woman wearing a thick coat and carrying a clipboard made her way toward Susanna, smiling. "We are ready for you to open the event. We have eager shoppers lined up at the south entrance of the park all the way down Market."

"Splendid." Susanna motioned to Avery. "Mrs. Woodrow, I'd like you to meet my sister, Avery Truitt."

"Miss Truitt, we're so glad you're here to help." The woman scanned her clipboard. "You're in the cupcake booth. Number fifteen."

"Me?"

"Her Majesty said it would be all right, that you'd want to volunteer."

"Yes, of course but—" Avery made a face at Susanna.

"Oh, come on, it'll be fun. You don't want to stand around, do you?"

Cupcake booth it is. She liked cupcakes. In fact, she made batches of them in college. It was her way of relaxing, bringing a bit of the Rib Shack life to central Ohio, to her friends and teammates. The male volleyball team certainly liked to stop by on cupcake night. Ha! Even *that* couldn't land her a man. "So, where do I go again?"

Avery glanced around the park, lined with booths amid the shoveled snow, and preteens and teens eager to get down to business.

"Booth number fifteen." Mrs. Woodrow pointed behind Avery. "Right over there. You'll be assisting Prince Colin."

CHAPTER 10

He eyed Avery as he moved past the fair officials, shaking hands, trying not to get waylaid. His suggestion to put Avery in the booth with him went over without a hitch. Mrs. Woodrow was none the wiser. He only hoped she didn't out him.

Be casual, mate. Just like when you met her the first time. "Hello." He greeted her outside the booth. "I hear you're with me in the cupcake stand."

"Odd coincidence."

"True enough." He reached for the low booth door. "But we cannot deny Mrs. Woodrow's clipboard." Was that a slight grin on the edge of her lips?

"I'm doing this for Susanna." Avery ducked into the booth after him.

"You have to put a shoulder to the wheel when in Brighton. Family helps family. Isn't that what you told me once when I visited St. Simons? You tied an apron around my neck and led me to the fry vat."

"You were a good fry man," she said.

He'd arrived on the island late one Friday evening, surprising her with a quick twenty-four-hour visit. A friend from uni had flown his father's private jet over and Colin convinced him to land in Savannah.

Her expression, the taste of her lips on his that night as they walked along the midnight beach, their toes sinking into cool, gritty sand, was worth the price he paid. Lack of sleep, earning a low mark on a paper due upon his return.

"A-are you expecting a lot of people? At this event?" Avery said, reaching for one of the aprons hanging from a hook on the bare plywood wall.

"I hope so. At least that's the goal."

Across the park, through the throng, protection officers watched the booth. Well-wishers, curious citizens, and the press slowed as they passed.

"Prince Colin, Peggy Monarch from the *Informant*." She leaned through the booth, her elbows on the counter. "Did you ring the bell for Lady Jordan? Say you did. We know it's so."

"Not today, Peggy."

He dodged the question with a wave and a chuckle, feeling the heat of Avery's presence beside him every step. He'd made up his mind to address this issue with her privately as they set up to sell cupcakes, but shoppers had already formed a queue.

"Here." Colin handed her a box of cupcakes. "I guess we can set them on the counter."

He hunched down as the low ceiling grazed the top of his head. Also ducking low, Avery handed him the other apron, looping it over his head.

"I'm not sure I can stand up in here."

"I don't plan to marry on Christmas Day," he said without preamble.

She barely glanced at him. "You don't owe me an explanation."

But he did. For himself. To have the record clear. "I just wanted you to know." He tied the apron strings around his coat.

"Fine. Now, what about these cupcakes?" Avery reached for several boxes, bonking her head twice. She patted her head, laughing. "I can't work in here."

Seeing the woman he fell for sprang open his senses. If there weren't a gaggle of people staring at them, he'd reach for her, inhale her scent, and tell her how much he'd missed her. The words soared and floated across his heart, but remained trapped behind the barrier of decorum.

"Can we have a cupcake? We'd like to keep moving. It's rather icy, Your Majesty."

"Just Colin, please . . ." He smiled, made a face at Avery. "Do you want to be in charge of the money? Or shall I?"

"You. I don't know a quid from a ha'penny."

He laughed. "Ha'penny? I've not heard that term in a long while. They ceased to be legal tender fifty years ago."

"You make my point." She found a metal box on the lower shelf and passed it to him. Inside he found coins and notes for making change. "I'm going to work outside." She held up two boxes of cupcakes. "How much?"

"They told me there'd be a price list." Colin searched the shelves of the booth. "Ah, here, four cupcakes for ten pounds. There're four to a box. All the money goes to the children."

"All right. We are good to go." Avery headed out.

Colin followed with the money box. "You hand out the boxes, I'll gather the money. Get these folks on their way."

He caught her as she started out, catching his breath when her brown eyes met his. "You believe me, don't you? I didn't ring the bell. Please, I need someone on my side."

She gave him a pinched expression. "I don't think it's any of my business."

"Prince Colin, please, leave the girl be. I want me cupcakes so I can get on me way."

Avery shot the boisterous woman a smile. "Coming right up." She passed over one of the boxes. "Here we are. Four for ten pounds. Hand your money to the prince."

Colin hurried to take the money, then worked the crowd with Avery. The protection officers scrambling alongside.

"You're a tall one."

Avery glanced down at the stout man sporting a winter beard. "And happy to be so."

Colin grinned, shaking his head, collecting money from the fairgoers, pausing often for selfies, the protection detail holding their protest even though the crowd thickened. But Avery was the real charmer. Not him. She was sincere and open, humble with no pretense, and the people felt it.

In short order, they doled out the boxes. Inside an hour, only a few boxes remained. Avery returned to the booth for two more boxes, handing Colin a wad of money. "They're handing it to me. I hope it's the right amount."

Colin shuffled through the bills. "Looks right. You know you could slow down and let me walk with you."

"Where's the fun in that?" She grinned, filling him with her warmth and light, his heart and mind pinging all over. If this kept up, he'd not need his coat. Never mind the cold and threat of snow.

She was too easy to be around. She stirred him. Made him want to shout to the world he still loved her.

The cupcake clamoring died suddenly so Avery walked the thoroughfare calling, "Cupcakes, get your cupcakes."

Several children gathered around, wanting one cupcake apiece. Avery broke open the box to serve them.

Then to Colin's wondering eyes, Guy Smoot appeared with Lady Sarah on his arm.

"I heard you were manning a booth, my man, but I dared not believe it." He gave his attention to Avery. "Do you remember me? Guy Smoot. It's been awhile."

She offered her hand. "Good to see you, Guy."

"This is Lady Sarah."

"Lovely to meet you," Sarah said, leaning against Guy. "I heard you were the one—"

"Who's helping me sell cupcakes." Colin hustled in between the women, cutting off Sarah. It was all coming back to him now that his friends from uni knew too much.

"Why don't you buy the last few boxes, Guy? Help the children." Colin took two boxes from Avery, shoving them at his friend.

"Hmm. . . ." Guy inspected the contents. "Seems rather ordinary, boring, just tossing a few quid at a box of cupcakes."

"Not everything has to bring the thrill of jumping from an airplane," Sarah said.

"Precisely. Finally, some wisdom." Colin motioned for Guy to pay up. "That'll be twenty pounds. If you don't want them, run them round to the senior home."

Guy retrieved a wad of money from his pocket. "I'll tell you what . . ." He peeled off a couple of notes. "Avery, how much for you to toss a cupcake at the prince? Hit him square in the face?"

Colin scoffed. "You've gone mad. Avery, don't listen to him."

"What do you think?" Guy removed another note from the roll in his hand. "Fifty pounds? A hundred?"

"Smoot, she's not hitting me with a cupcake."

"Fine, two hundred pounds, but you have to hit him square between the eyes."

"This is ridiculous." Did Guy mean to vex him on such a glorious day? "Avery, pay him no mind."

"Deal." She snatched the money from Guy before he could crack a smile. "Two hundred quid. One cupcake. Right between the eyes."

"Tally-ho, Avery. Well done, lass. But best let me hold on to the money. Just in case you miss."

"Oh, I won't miss." She passed the money to Colin. "Put it in the box."

This was madness. Surely she was not going to pelt him with a cupcake. "Avery, if you think I'm going to stand here and—"

"Put this on." Avery slipped her apron over her head. "Tuck it around your neck, you know, in case I do miss." Her cocky grin set his pulse to throbbing. "Can't have icing soiling your cashmere coat."

"You're serious?"

"Get that apron on because I'm throwing whether you're ready or not."

Then he saw it. The twinkle in her eye. The spark he loved so much. She needed to do this. And he needed to let her.

"Gather around everyone," Guy called, waving to passersby. "Prince Colin has agreed to be a target for charity. Two hundred pounds if this star American athlete hits him between the eyes with a cupcake."

Shouts and hoots rose from the people as they scurried close for the show.

"I'll put a fiver on that." A man from the back waved his money around.

"How grand! Anyone else?" Sarah went into motion, calling for and collecting more money. "It's for the children."

"I just want to lodge my formal protest," Colin said, opting to shed his coat before covering up with the aprons, storing his coat and the money in the booth. The brisk air soaked through his shirt-sleeves and the falling snow almost had a joyful jaunt.

"Come on, it'll be fun." Avery slipped from her coat, too, revealing her long, lean frame wrapped in a fitted blue dress. "I promise to make it a clean shot," she said, passing her coat to Sarah, then leaning his way, bringing the full force of her presence. The power of her presence crashed against him.

She flustered him. He couldn't think, and his ability to work an apron tie completely vanished.

"Need help?" Guy, laughing, taunted.

"No, mate, I got it."

Muttering, he fixed the apron round his neck and shoulders. If ever he doubted his affection for Avery, he only needed to remember this moment. She bewitched him.

"Ready?" She was so close he could feel the heat from her skin. One step forward and his body would be against hers. He ached with the desire, to hold her, to kiss her. "I promise to hit you right between the eyes."

"You're sure of yourself? I'm not sure the star of the cricket team could boast such a feat."

"Well, of course not." Laughing, teasing, Avery backed up, her frosted weapon in hand. Guy instructed her as to the distance he required, making a line in the snow with his gloved hand.

The spectators were so thick Colin's view across the park was obscured. Folks held up their phones. Their voices were like verbal percussion.

This was going to be humiliating. Unless she missed. Oh, why did he have a feeling she'd not miss?

"All right ole chap," Guy called. "We're ready."

Seeing the distance, Colin relaxed. Avery was a stellar athlete, but she was not going to pelt him between the eyes at that distance. Colin smoothed his hand down his chest, checking to make sure the apron covered the entirety of his shirt. He'd just purchased it for the season.

"Fire when ready, Avery." He wasn't even going to close his eyes. He wanted to be wide-eyed and watching when her efforts plopped on the snow way short.

Avery stepped to the line, the cupcake in her palm. She eyed Colin. Studied the distance. Pretended to check the wind. Surveyed the shower of snowflakes.

"Getting cold, Avery," Colin taunted her. "Anytime now. But if you're—"

The next second dropped into slow motion. Avery reared back like an American baseball player, firing the chocolate-frosted bomb like a shot. Colin saw every inch as it traveled to his face.

He drew half a breath before the thing smacked him square between the eyes and stuck there, the stump of a sweet frosted horn. The crowd went wild, cheering, laughing, thumping Avery on the back, against the will of the protection officers.

"Fantastic. Incredible." Guy ran toward Colin, his phone aimed, snapping one photo after another. "Avery, that was brilliant. Best money I've spent in a good long while."

Colin tipped his head to the ground, waiting for the cupcake to fall off, feeling the slow release of the stick frosting. "Now, can we sell these cupcakes proper—"

"Who's next?" Guy said. "Step right up. You, too, can have your shot at the prince."

"Me, me." A woman cut through the crowd. "Never thought I'd see the likes of this. And seeing the prince is a true sport, why not take a shot?"

"Guy—"

But it was too late. The queue was forming as Sarah collected the money while Avery collected the final cupcake boxes.

"You don't mind, do you?" she whispered, pausing to wipe frosting from his forehead. "There're only four boxes left."

He peered at her, her brownish-golden gaze extinguishing the fight within him. "No, I don't mind at all."

So Colin spent the next hour being pelted by perfectly fine cupcakes. More and more fairgoers stepped up, and when the cupcakes ran out, Avery recycled those that fell short.

The last customer was Colin's favorite, and maybe worth the whole ordeal. A darling three-year-old with curly ponytails wanted her shot at the prince. So Colin crouched down, allowing her to smash a slightly used cupcake against his nose.

Her laugh was worth his humiliation. Afterward he posed with her for a photograph, covered in frosting—chocolate, vanilla, and strawberry. Most of it on his apron, but a lot in his hair and on his face.

"You are a sport among sportsmen," Guy trumpeted, handing

a pile of money to Avery, bowing to Colin. "I can't remember when I've had a better time."

"Well, I can." Colin gingerly removed the apron around his neck, finding a clean edge to wipe down his face.

"Colin, you were magnificent." Sarah kissed his very sweet cheek. "And delicious. Guy, let's visit Franklin's. I'm in the mood for a cupcake."

Guy and Sarah disappeared across the thoroughfare. Colin was alone with Avery and two rather perturbed protection officers.

"Hey . . ." Avery leaned to see his face, gently knocking a bit of frosting from his hair. "It's a good thing most of them were not good shots. You'd be nothing but cake and icing."

Gingerly, with ease, he removed the second apron. "Guy Smoot has not heard the last of this."

Avery took the aprons from him, carefully folding them so more crumbs wouldn't fall to the already cupcaked snow. "Come on, you had fun and you know it." A confidence flickered across her gaze. "You were a hero this afternoon."

"Was I? Does that make you and Guy the villains?"

"If you want." She walked back to the booth, setting the aprons on the counter. "Is there a trash can around here? We need to clean this up."

"Over there." Colin started for the bin by the trees, the winter evening beginning to cloak the city.

The sight was beautiful. He paused, gripping the trash bin. Christmas in Cathedral City was glorious. Colorful. Joyful. Lights glittering from store fronts, from loft apartments.

But the air was brisk and Avery waited. Colin headed back to the booth, dragging the bin behind him, the amber glow of the park lights highlighting his path. Highlighting his heart.

Was there a better place on earth to be than in Maritime Park with Avery Truitt, the Christmas season upon them?

Back at the booth, Avery worked a broom over the snow, gathering the cupcake debris, giggling to herself.

"Is it still so funny?"

"Yes."

He exhaled, grinning. "Guess it must have been quite the sight."

Avery leaned on her broom, laughing, her boot heels digging into the snow. "I'm hopping on YouTube as soon as I get home."

Colin shook his head, grinning. He liked making her laugh. "This will be well worth it if you told me we made more than a thousand pounds." He scooped cake and frosting into the bin. What a mess.

"I don't have the total, but we did well."

"Your Majesty, please . . ." Men dressed in park grounds uniforms hurried toward him. "We're on detail. No need for you to wield a broom." A large man with a thick brow took the device from Colin.

"Indeed." The other man hovered over Avery. "Miss, please, we can take things from here."

She passed over her broom, returning to the booth. "I guess I'd better go. Susanna will be wondering where I am."

"I'm sure she knows. The protection officers are in touch the entire time." In the booth, Colin slung his coat over his shoulder. He'd not soil the silk lining with his sticky shirt sleeves. "Ready to go?"

She regarded him as she slipped into her coat. "Wait." She reached for his hair. "You still have icing stuck to your hair."

Lowering his head for her to get a good look, Colin spied a lone cupcake in the corner of the booth counter. *Well, hello, little friend. Two can play the cupcake game.*

Carefully reaching behind him, he scooped up the cupcake, holding it behind his back as Avery worked frosting from his hair.

"You're going to have to scrub hard to get this one out." She chuckled and moved an inch closer, her fragrance teasing all of Colin's senses. After a moment, she lowered her arm but remained in his space. "Th-thank you for today. It . . . it was fun. I needed a good laugh."

"Me too." Colin raised his free hand slowly to her cheek, then down her neck, brushing aside the long loose curls of her hair. At the right moment, *smash*, he'd deliver the cupcake right to her face.

"Colin . . ." she said, resting her hand on his arm. "What are you doing?"

"Looking at you. Beautiful. Confident. Invincible." The cupcake wavered in his hand.

Her smile melted his bones. "You were the people's prince today. You . . . you really are amazing, Colin." Her eyes met his for only a second, then she glanced away, as if her confession wasn't meant to be spoken out loud.

"Why does it sound so true when you say it?"

"Truth is truth, you know that. You know it when you hear it."

"Remember the first time I took you home?" he said, tipping his head to see her eyes. "Well, when I took you back to Parrsons House? When you were guests of the queen for Nathaniel's coronation?"

"We'd been at your house all evening, watching movies with your friends and sisters, eating your mama out of house and home."

"I held your hand as I walked you out to my car." Colin stepped closer, lacing his cold fingers with hers.

"We both went for the passenger door and bumped heads."

"You started laughing."

"Only because you were so sure you had a knot on your head." She brushed her fingers over his forehead, her soft touch sparking all kinds of flames. "You tried to see in the side mirror, but the night was too dark."

"We had the moonlight, though."

"Then I inspected your head for a bump. Just in case. Couldn't take you back to Aunt Campbell's house wounded."

It was in the thin wisps of moonlight, they stood eye to eye, nose to nose as he'd swept his thumbs over her forehead.

"I don't see anything . . ." But what did he know? Her presence consumed every part of him. "Except your beautiful face."

"You're flirting with me."

"I am." He slipped his hands down her arms, linking his fingers through hers. "I sure didn't expect you when I heard a couple of American friends of Nathaniel's were coming to the coronation."

"What did you expect?"

"I don't know, but nothing like you came to mind."

"You didn't expect a tall girl with skinny legs?" She baited him. Dared him to expose his intimate thoughts.

"I didn't expect a sweet, funny, beautiful, kind of sexy lass—"

"Kind of? Please, Colin, you bowl me over with that kind of talk."

He laughed, tightening his fingers around hers. "Well, if I said completely sexy you'd think me a cad. Rightfully so. Besides, I'm thinking of your dad back home. I don't want him to hate me before he meets me."

She stood away from him. "You want to meet my dad?"

"I do." Right then and there he lost his heart to her.

Colin tapped her chin with his fingertip and raised her face to his. Without another word, he gave her a chaste and tender kiss, lightly running his hand along the base of her neck.

"Prince Colin?" A masculine voice ripped him from the memory, from Avery's warm breath on his skin. He glanced round to see the protection officer extending through the booth window. "Hurry along, sir. The princess is ready to go."

"We'll be along." He let the cupcake topple from his hand to the snowy and muddy booth floor.

"Colin, let's go." Avery reached for her handbag, but in one fluttering moment, Colin slipped his arm around her and drew her close. He searched her expression for a yes or a no, wanting to kiss her.

Another flutter and he lowered his lips to hers, his pulse a surging rhythm.

His first touch was light, tentative. Would she slap him? But when Avery raised her arms to his neck, inhaling, everything loving and true about her vibrated through him. He gripped her tighter, pressing his lips into a wanting kiss.

Suddenly the kiss ended, Avery shifting backward. "Colin—" She touched her fingers to her lips, ducking out the booth door. "I need to go."

"Avery, wait—"

He chased her as she dashed out of the booth, love pounding in his heart. He'd endure a thousand cupcake peltings to be in her presence, to hear her laugh, to kiss her again.

But to make such a declaration might cost him everything.

CHAPTER 11

December 7
Eighteen days until Christmas

In the bright gymnasium of a local school, Avery hunkered down on the sidelines, watching the girls practice.

A surprise invitation had arrived from the coach at a nearby academy late yesterday afternoon through Susanna's office.

We formally invite Miss Avery to view our practice.
We're a young team, just beginning a girls' volleyball side.
If she's agreeable, we could use some pointers.
Sincerely,
Isobel Rudolf

Susanna didn't have to read the invitation to Avery twice. She welcomed the opportunity. Welcomed the chance to touch a bit of reality, her life after the Christmas season. Welcomed the chance to stop thinking of Colin, going over and over the feel of his arm around her back, the warm sensation of his kiss. So potent was his touch she dreamed of him.

They'd not talked since she dashed away. It was for the best. She was on the verge of saying something she couldn't retract, like, "I love you."

Being in his world, even for a few days, made her realize what an impossible match they would be. He involved with the family business with an eye toward politics. She with a desire to coach. Spread new wings in the sporting world.

"That's good, Meredith," Avery called to the girl at setter. "Get under the ball. Don't be afraid."

"What do you think of her in that position?" Coach Rudolf leaned over Avery's shoulder.

"She's got the height and athletic ability, Isobel. But . . ." Avery pressed her hand over her heart. "She needs courage. She's timid. A setter needs good leadership and communication skills."

"Agree. But she has good hands and is such a student of the game."

"Have her command the court, call the ball, direct traffic. Force her to use her knowledge of the game."

Isobel nodded. "I've played for years, but coaching is new to me. You seem a natural. Can I take you to tea and pick your brain?"

"I can come to practice again tomorrow if you'd like."

"Could you? This is our last week until the new year. We have a short spring season coming. First one for this team." The coach headed for the bleachers, calling the girls after her.

Avery took a seat, listening as Isobel pep-talked the girls, reminding them all, "You can do it if you just believe in yourselves."

A flutter skipped through Avery and she battled the urge to

shove the coach aside and cheer the girls herself. She could do this. She wanted to do this.

Isobel dismissed the girls and joined Avery on the bleachers. "Thank you for coming. It means a lot."

"Thank you for asking."

"I follow American college volleyball. Couldn't believe my luck when I read you were here all month with your mum."

"My dad died in June. Mama wanted the family to be together for the Christmas season."

"I'm so sorry for your loss. Perhaps the beauty of Cathedral City at Christmastime will ease your sorrows."

Avery smiled. "Thank you. I'm sure it will."

Isobel gazed off, her expression one of remembering. "I had a tour of the palace once, when I was in school. It had all us girls dreaming of marrying a prince." She glanced back at Avery. "Did your sister dream of marrying a prince?"

"Nope. She wanted to marry her high school boyfriend. In fact, she met Nathaniel the night her boyfriend said, and I quote, 'I found the right ring but not the right girl.'"

"What?" Isobel appeared appropriately appalled. "He actually said that? I hope the princess punched him in the nose."

Avery laughed low. "She should've, but she realized he was right. Best thing that ever happened to her."

"What about you, miss? I see the papers. You and Prince Colin? Tossing cupcakes?" Isobel wasn't shy, was she? "What was that about?"

"I had nothing to do with it. Well, except to throw the first cupcake. But his friend Guy Smoot put up two hundred pounds for charity. Then everyone else wanted a shot at him."

Isobel's laugh was sweet. "Wish I'd been there. That Prince Colin is quite the sport."

"Y-yes, he is." For a few minutes, she'd purged him from her thoughts. He was back now, center court.

The headlines after the fund-raiser were full of speculation. The *LibP* headline read, "Prince Colin and American Avery Truitt. Is There Another 'Georgia Belle' for the Royal Family?"

The accompanying photograph showed Avery wrapped in his arms, her head back laughing, Colin's gaze fixed on her, a big ole grin lighting up his perfect profile.

She didn't remember being in his arms except for the kiss. But the moment she saw the image on the newsprint, her heart declared, "Now, there is a couple in love."

But they weren't in love. Their season had passed.

"He's thick with Lady Jordan Skye, though, isn't he?" Isobel fished without bait. Just a bare, honest hook.

"So, tomorrow then?" Avery stood to go, reaching for her coat, nodding to the protection officer waiting in the corner. Avoidance was the best defense. "Three o'clock?"

"Yes, thank you so much. See you then."

In the car ride back to the palace, Avery watched Cathedral City slip by, straining to feel the Christmas spirit floating through the city. But thoughts of Colin awakened anxieties.

The car passed a cathedral. A banner waved in the wind, tickled by the red fingers of the setting sun.

"Unto *us* a child is born . . ."

Avery powered down her window and stretched out over the door. The arched and ribbed structure of the ancient church reminded her this season was about more than shops and lights, wrappings and ribbons, about more than a Christmas tree and carols, about more than cozy nights by the fire watching her favorite Christmas classic. It was about more than feelings.

It was about God becoming a baby, growing into a man who endured a cross for *her* sins. She watched the banner go by, the wind tangling through her hair, the cold burning her cheeks.

God, You got this, don't You? You got me.

Seemed if He went to all the trouble to send Jesus as a baby with the express purpose of redeeming mankind through the ugly cross, He'd have a purpose in mind for Avery.

The driver slowed the car at the palace gate to punch in the security code. Avery ducked back into the car. She had to trust in God. What choice did she have? Worrying away her life? No thanks.

As the car eased through the gates toward the palace, she scanned her e-mail. Hey! One of her teammates got engaged. Way to go, Bailey.

No response from UCLA, but did she really want to live twenty-five hundred miles from home? Even that much farther from Colin?

Avery shifted in her seat. *Come on now, forget him.* The memory of his kiss surfaced again. That very luscious kiss. *Nope, not going there.* Back to e-mail, she scanned to the bottom, about to put her phone away, when something caught her eye. She sat forward with a good thump of her heart.

The subject line read "Interview Request from Valdosta State."

Trembling, she scanned the e-mail as the car descended under the arches into the garage.

> We cordially invite you for an interview as assistant volleyball coach. As the semester is winding down, we'd like to set a date for Tuesday, December 13. Please respond if this is convenient for you.

Hit Reply. Why hesitate?

Thank you for the invitation. December 13 would be
perfect for me.

A job. She had a job interview. The protection officer opened
her car door. "I got a job interview, Lynell."

"Good for you, miss."

"Yay! Good for me."

Avery hurried to her suite, then to find Mama and Susanna,
tell them the good news. She'd be gone for a couple of days, but
when she came back, she just might be a college volleyball coach.

See? While she was busy surrendering her future to God, He
was already putting things into motion.

She hesitated just outside Susanna's apartment door, staring
down at her phone. Should she? Why not? Without too much con-
sideration, she sent Colin a text.

Got a job interview at Valdosta State. Tuesday. Wish me
luck.

CHAPTER 12

December 8
Seventeen days until Christmas

Madeline & Hyacinth Live! Show

Madeline: "For all of you keeping track of the
Christmas Day wedding on our bell app,
we've had little to no activity since the
cupcake war photos three days ago. Come
on now, let's not lose hope already."

Hyacinth: "Our staff dug up some of the traditional
wooing gifts of past bell ringers. (She read from
a blue card.) Here's my favorite . . . a male and
female goat. (The audience laughed.) Some sort
of dowry, I suppose. So, our dear viewers, if you
hear the bleating of goats going down Galloway
Boulevard to Lady Jordan's place, please text
us. Hashtag #princecolinrangthebell."

Madeline: (Laughing) "Surely the prince will not be sending goats to her gorgeous apartment building. I'm not sure they'd allow them in."

Hyacinth: "When true love is afoot, no telling what a man will do. (facing the camera) Prince Colin, send goats. I'd love it if you did. How old world!"

Madeline: (Laughing) "How do you like the American Avery Truitt for the object of Prince Colin's affection? (pointing to an image behind her) Do you think this picture means anything?"

Hyacinth: "They look mighty cozy, those two. But look, she's not really holding on to him." (Hyacinth circles Avery's hands with a laser pointer.) "He's got a loose hold on her. I think they're friends." (She made a face, waving off the photo and its implications.) "Nothing to see here, ladies and gents. Move along."

Madeline: "So we're still hoping for a Prince Colin and Lady Jordan match at Watchman Abbey Christmas morn. (The audience cheered.) Hy, you remember now that part of the tradition is the wooed woman does not give her answer until Christmas morning."

Hyacinth: "Precisely. She'll show or not. The man is completely vulnerable."

Madeline: "I can't imagine—"

Hyacinth: "—anything more romantic."

Madeline: "I was going to say scary, but we'll go with your word. For now." (tapping Hyacinth's blue card) "Read the rest of the bell ringer's wooing gifts."

Hyacinth: "Here's one of my favorites.
A decorated fir tree."

Madeline: "That'd be really sweet."

Hyacinth: "A bolt of fine cloth."

Madeline: "Perhaps for making the wedding dress?"

Hyacinth: "Dried meat and spices."

Madeline: "Of course, for the bridal dinner. The
groom has to provide a reception. It was
the tradition a hundred years ago."

Hyacinth: "Leather."

Madeline: (Making a face) "For? Oh, luggage.
Of course! For the honeymoon."

(Hyacinth slapped her a high five.)

Hyacinth: "Now, that's my kind of man. Goes
and prepares the wedding, the reception,
the honeymoon for his bride." (She looked
at the camera.) "Prince Colin, if you're
watching, I think you have a pretty clear set
of marching orders. Go get your bride."

Madeline: "Stay tuned. We'll be right back after this."

December 9
Sixteen days until Christmas

Snow drifted from a slate gray sky hovering over Cathedral
City. This was ridiculous. He'd read the same line of the
contract a dozen times. Still didn't understand it. In an hour he'd
be in a meeting where his father expected his input on this deal,

but all he could remember was Avery and the feel of her form against his.

Shoving away from his desk, he stood and peered out the window, slipping his phone from his pocket. Tapping the screen, he opened his messages and read the two-day-old text from Avery. Again.

Got a job interview at Valdosta State. Tuesday. Wish me luck.

He'd responded with, Cheering you on. But it was a lie. A bold-faced lie.

He didn't want her in Georgia. He wanted her here. She'd taken up residence in his mind, his heart, and he couldn't seem to move her out.

The picture in the paper didn't help. Normally he winced at such reports, but the image of Avery in his arms spoke to him.

She belonged there.

The *Sun Tattler* theorized Colin was trying to move speculation away from Lady Jordan. The *Informant* suggested he wanted to make the Lady of the Screen jealous.

Neither. He'd refused calls from reporters, so he had to endure their postulating. Truth was he'd not seen Jordan since the Harvest Celebration. Which was so very typical for them. He called her a week later and her voice mail picked up.

He expected as much. Thought she'd been furious about the bell ringing and made no effort to hide her feelings, even after he dropped her home around one a.m.

"I really hope you're not planning to propose, Colin. I'm filming a new movie in London."

"Trust me, that's the last thing on my mind."

At least with her.

A light knock echoed from his door and Dad peeked round. "Might I have a moment?"

"Sure." Colin moved back to his desk but remained standing.

He liked these moments when Dad popped round for advice, seeking his insight or opinion.

"Palmer Charles called. The unions in the Hessenberg plant are working toward a strike. He's asked me to come to negotiations. He's sure my presence will go a long way to calm the waters."

"I agree," Colin said. Dad was a diplomat's diplomat.

"That being so, I need you to take my place in the Casting Finance Group board meeting next week."

"In New York?" Colin stepped around his desk. He'd be in America the same time as Avery.

"Indeed. Get with Eden on flight and hotel." Dad handed over a dossier. "You'll need to review this before the vote. Remember to keep Tattersall interests foremost in your mind." He reached for the contract Colin couldn't seem to manage. "What are your thoughts on this?"

"The margins are—"

"Too narrow?"

"Yes." Sounded like a good answer.

"Agree. They gave Shomberg Co. a way better deal." Dad smiled from the door. "Have fun in New York. Take an extra day or two, see the sights. Maybe Christmas shop. Your sisters would love a gift from Tiffany's."

"All right. I guess I can knock around Manhattan for a day or two on my own."

"Perhaps you could invite Lady Jordan along."

"Dad . . . no. The press would be all over it. And you know how I feel about—"

"Yes, you and your old-fashioned ways. I don't know how you manage to abstain. Consider Jordan as a good traveling companion. The company will spring for a separate room. Never know, you might just realize you are in love. Think of it, Colin, a prince married on Christmas Day, in Watchman Abbey. It will make the history books."

Dad's underlying tension with the royal family reverberated in his voice, in his desire to one-up them. To get back at Uncle Leo, may he rest in peace, for initially denying peerage to Sir Edward and Princess Louisa's offspring.

But to suggest he marry a woman he didn't love? Surely Dad did not wish it upon his eldest and heir. He'd not mentioned the picture of him with Avery.

"See you in a few," Dad said.

Colin picked up the contract, reading the first line again, not caring about margins and deals. He snapped up his phone.

Colin: Just found out I'll be in NYC while you're in Georgia.

Avery: Business or pleasure?

Colin: Business.

Avery: Good luck.

Colin: Yeah, you too.

He set down his phone, thinking it was more than fortunate he'd suddenly be in America the same time as Avery. Even though Georgia was a long way from New York.

He checked the time, then launched the Internet. He'd make his own arrangements for New York. With a little detour to his favorite Georgia island.

December 13
Twelve days until Christmas

The tour of Valdosta State's facility inspired her. She could see herself here. She flew overnight from Cathedral City and arrived on St. Simon's Monday midmorning.

She crashed in her room until the sun went down, then headed to the Shack for dinner. Being at home alone with no Christmas decorations was too depressing.

In the meantime, UCLA wrote to say they'd filled the position. One less choice to worry over.

"What do you think?" Coach Boon ended the tour in the gymnasium, hands on his waist. "Think you could work here?"

"Absolutely." The question boded well for Avery. It meant Coach was seriously considering her.

"The pay's not much, but it's decent, will give you a good start." He motioned to the bleachers. "Want to join the AD and my graduate assistant?"

Coach introduced Avery to the athletic director, an imposing former girls' basketball star from Connecticut named Dorian Smith, and the graduate assistant, Jason Medwin, a former player at Penn State.

"Coach tells us you're the one for the job, Avery." The AD got to the point.

"I'd love to be a part of this program. I'm Georgia born and raised. My family is just up the road on St. Simons Island."

"But you played college ball for the Big Ten," Dorian said.

"I liked Ohio State's program."

"You were Big Ten Player of the Year two years in a row." This from Jason, reading her stat sheet. "Leading in kills." He glanced up. "Looks to me like you worked hard."

"Is there any other way?"

The questions went round-robin, Avery answering probes about her career, her philosophies on coaching, and her injury.

"Your coaches speak very highly of you." The AD stood, backing away from the bleachers. "Coach Boon will take it from here."

Jason shook her hand. "It was great to meet you."

Coach Boon motioned for Avery to follow him back to his office. "You impressed them, Avery. I could tell."

Glad someone could. "So where to from here?"

"Dorian, Jason, and I will talk, go over the other candidates, but as far as I'm concerned"—Coach shot her a wide grin—"You've got the job. You'd be great for the team. The girls are aggressive, skilled, eager to learn. Just like you."

"Really? That would be amazing. I really want this job, Coach," Avery said, grabbing hold of her future with both hands. "I-I'm hungry for this."

"I heard your daddy died . . . Your high school coach mentioned it when I called for a reference. My condolences. Lost my dad when I was only thirty."

"Do you ever stop missing him?"

He chuckled softly. "He and I . . . were cut from the same cloth. Butted heads more than I'd like to remember. But yes, it gets better. Sad thing about losing your parent is a door to your childhood closes. One you didn't even know was open."

Avery glanced away, not wanting the coach to see the emotion rising in her eyes. "You . . . you just said in a few words what I've been wrestling with since his funeral."

"What would your old pop say? Would he want you at Valdosta State?"

She laughed, brushing a rebel tear from the corner of her eye. "He'd say 'Go get 'em, Ace.'"

"Then let's make it happen."

In her car, Avery fired up the engine and cranked the radio, tuning to a local station's Christmas rotation.

"Joy to the world/the Lord has come . . ."

The encounter with Coach healed her a bit. Filled the void in her soul that longed for a conversation with Daddy. Excited, she headed back to St. Simons and dinner at the Shack.

So this was what trusting in God and moving on felt like. Good. Positive. In fact, she'd return to Brighton with a fresh hope this Christmas season.

Replaying the interview in her mind, Avery felt good about her rapport with the AD and the graduate assistant. Believed her answers to their questions were solid.

By the time she pulled into the Rib Shack, she was jazzed, though jet lag seeped into her bones. Tonight would be a glorious sleep. But first, she wanted a plate of barbecue ribs, fries, green beans, and Daddy's perfect biscuits with black raspberry jam. She'd wash it all down with a tall, icy sweet tea. Her stomach rumbled at the very thought.

The best part about getting this job? She'd be free of Colin. What did she care about the bell ringing? If he married *Lady* Jordan Skye? Good for him. She suited the life he had planned more than Avery.

A laugh echoed in her chest as the image of him covered

with cupcake icing rose to her consciousness. Such a nice parting memory. After learning the truth behind his rejection, pelting him with a cupcake gave her a sense of vindication. Even the kiss—a shiver ran through her middle—proved to be the perfect consolation. She could remember him fondly now. Why he stood her up was a thing of the past. At last.

Breezing through the kitchen's back door, Avery dropped her jacket and purse in Mama's office.

"Bristol, I'm starved. House special, please."

"Coming up." Lean and pretty, Bristol had been at the Shack since Avery could remember. She was family. "How'd it go?" She shoved two plates through the window, under the heat lamp. "Jasmine, table five."

"Amazing. I'm 99 percent sure I have a job." Avery picked a warm biscuit from the tray and popped open the lowboy for a jelly packet. "I really liked the coach. Could tell he liked me."

"Of course he liked you." Bristol slid a plate across the prep table toward Avery. "Your mama will be tickled to have you close to home."

"You should see her in Brighton, Bristol. She's her old self." Avery collected a roll of silverware, then dragged around a stool, pausing, glancing to Daddy's station at the stove.

"That warms my heart. I wondered if she'd ever get over losing Gib. Shoot, I still miss him, Aves."

"Me too. I'd love to talk to him about this job."

"Guess you can talk to the heavenly Father." Bristol set a tall tea in front of Avery, then leaned against the prep table. "So, tell me, girl, have you seen Prince Colin?"

Bristol had walked with Avery through the painful summer of silence and rejection. They spent a lot of late nights out on the deck, after the Rib Shack closed, talking, downing too much sweet tea and caffeine.

"I've seen him. And he's seen me." Avery reached for the salt and a bottle of ketchup, then pulled her phone from her pocket, opening to a picture from the *LibP*. "I hit him in the face with a cupcake. For a fund-raiser."

"You're kidding." Bristol laughed, immediately frowning when she saw the picture. "What's this? You look like an in-love couple. And where's this cupcake hit you speak of?"

"Swipe the screen. Next shot."

Bristol laughed. "Now that's more like it. But—" She returned to the first photo. "What's this about? Hmm?"

"Nothing . . . just . . ." A moment caught in a wrinkle of time she couldn't remember. "Anyway, he told me why he canceled on prom."

"Unless he was knocking on death's door, there is no excuse."

Avery relayed Colin's story. His father was against the relationship. His studies suffered. And he had a long road ahead of him with university and naval training. He was spending too much money.

"Hogwash. Pure hogwash." Bristol turned back to the window, putting up plates Catfish served. "LuEllen, table six." She faced Avery, hand on her hip. "That boy loved you. Everyone could see it."

Avery picked up a barbecue rib, the aroma stirring her longing for Daddy more than her taste buds. "We were too young."

"Young, smung. You loved each other. Everyone could see it. Your parents were young when they married."

"That's your example? They fought so bad they scared the wits out of Susanna. Then they got divorced."

"But then they found Jesus and got remarried. Had you."

"Bristol, it's too late for Colin and me." Avery motioned to the dining room. "Why aren't the Christmas decorations up yet? There're only twelve days til Christmas."

"Ain't no time. That's the one thing we miss about you and your mama being here. Catfish and I just can't seem to get to it."

"Why don't I do it?"

"Darling, if you could do that for me, I'd love you forever."

"You'll love me forever even if I don't do it. But tomorrow I'll get this place decorated. Turn it into a winter wonderland."

Digging into her dinner, Avery read an incoming message from Susanna. A new designer friend of hers wanted to dress Avery for the Christmas ball on the twenty-eighth.

You're home on Friday, right? Please be ready Sat. morning for a fitting. She's going on old measurements from a gown of mine. I told her you were taller. Thinner. Oh, Aves, I saw the material. It's gorgeous.

Avery hit reply. I'll be ready.

And she would. She'd not let her sister down. What was not to love about a Christmas Ball in a gorgeous designer, one-of-a-kind gown?

Another bite of her ribs and fries and she shoved her plate away. Jet lag kicked in and her appetite gave way to weariness. Sipping her tea, she watched Catfish and Bristol work, sensing her excitement over the job starting to wane. *You're just tired.* But Bristol's voice resounded in her head.

"You two loved each other."

Avery shifted around on the stool, facing the dining room, battling the growing sensation she was about to settle for good instead of the best.

CHAPTER 13

December 14
Eleven days until Christmas

There's a reason they call them board meetings. They're boring. Nothing but numbers, corporate speak, and boisterous predictions.

But Colin had triumphed, completed his obligation, and wined and dined the board members on his corporate credit card. Then he walked the streets along Times Square, lost among the crowd and the crazies, stood across the street from Saks Fifth Avenue watching a light show of snowflakes dancing across the side of the giant store.

Wednesday he walked the Avenue of the Americas. Admired the tree in Rockefeller Center, contemplated a turn around the ice rink but opted for lunch at a diner instead, checked his watch, and at four o'clock hailed a cab.

He had a plane to catch.

The two-and-a-half-hour flight landed him in Jacksonville around eight. He rented a car and drove an hour up to St. Simons.

First stop, the Truitt place to check for Avery. She wasn't there so Colin headed for the Rib Shack.

He caught his reflection in the rearview mirror of his rental car. This was madness, right? He had no idea how she'd respond to his surprise.

Should he telephone? Yes, he should ring her. But what difference would it make? He was here. And he didn't come all this way to talk to her on his mobile.

Though, if he really considered his actions, he wasn't sure why he was here or what he wanted. Just that he had to see her. And maybe tell her the rest of the story.

Wednesday Evening

Bing Crosby crooned a velvety "Silent Night" as Avery dragged the box of ornaments across the freshly mopped dining room floor.

She'd put up the Christmas tree this morning, but lost the rest of the day when she filled in for one of the servers. But now it was time to decorate.

The front-of-house crew bugged out twenty minutes after closing. In the back, Bristol and Catfish cleaned up and prepped for tomorrow.

"Avery, turn up them Christmas carols," Catfish called to the tune of banging and clanging pots.

"Coming right up." Avery reached into the utility closet behind the cash register and upped the jukebox volume.

"Sleep in heavenly peace . . ."

During the afternoon lull, Avery had managed to string the lights along the windows and around the checkout counter. The busboys caught the spirit and strung colored lights and garland along the back deck. And the servers set a wreath at the end of each table.

Now she sorted through the ornaments, humming, *"It's beginning to look a lot like Christmas."*

The first ornament out of the box was one she made for Daddy when she was in first grade. A wooden Santa with a fluffy white painted beard. On the back, she'd written in crayon, "For Daddy, by Avery Truitt, 6 years old."

She knelt by the box, tears welling, and kissed the crudely crafted piece. Daddy hung this one every year.

"You helped to save us, Aves. Your mama and me. I dare say Susanna. We were lost and wounded until Jesus met us head-on. Then He gave us you, and well . . . there's so much healing in a newborn life."

Avery touched the thin particle board with the edge of her finger.

"Merry Christmas, Daddy." She hung the wooden Santa on the center branch. Little by little, it was starting to look a lot like Christmas.

In the quiet hollow between Bing's last note and the next song on the jukebox's Christmas selections, Bristol's and Catfish's voices rose from the back of house along with the clanging and banging of dishes and lowboy doors.

Andy Williams crooned a new song into the Rib Shack. *"O holy night/the stars are brightly shining . . ."*

And Avery adorned the tree with Mama's very eclectic ornament collection—gorgeous ceramic redbirds swinging from a branch next to a plastic surfing Santa whose surfboard sled was guided by eight pink flamingos.

Beauty meets the beast.

"Christ is the Lord / O praise His name forever."

The melody and lyric provoked her. Closing her eyes, Avery tapped her hand to her heart, remembering the sign in Brighton. *"Unto us a son is born."*

He'd given up the splendor of heaven for the yuck of earth, endured the brutality of the cross to demonstrate perfect love. To give her life meaning and purpose.

So why did she feel so torn and confused? The perfect job awaited her. At just the right time. But she'd tossed and turned all night, drifting to sleep, then bolting awake with her heart pounding.

She dug in the ornament box for the crystal cross and hung it next to a ceramic manger. How could one observe Christmas without recognizing the cross?

The music crescendoed, pushing Avery out of melancholy into a place of faith.

Why the turmoil? Because getting a real job meant *it* was over—all hope of *ever* picking up with Colin again. She didn't realize until this moment she'd harbored such a desire.

"O Holy Night" faded away and Andy returned with a rousing rendition. *"It's the most wonderful time of the year . . ."*

Avery joined in the chorus, dropping ornaments on faux fir limbs, singing at the top of her lungs in a voice only a surfing Santa should hear.

When she came around the side of the tree, she stopped cold. Colin stood on the edge of the dining room by the kitchen.

"Oh my gosh, you scared me." She pressed her hand to her thumping heart. "Colin, what are you doing here?"

"I hope you don't mind." He motioned to the kitchen's swinging door. "Bristol let me in."

"No, i-it's fine." She peered at the kitchen, making a face as Bristol peeked through the service window. He was lucky she didn't give him a swift kick. "But, um, you know, Colin, you heard me sing, and well, now I might have to kill you."

He laughed. She exhaled.

"You sounded grand to me." He slipped from his jacket, a camel-colored suede. He looked good. As always. His thick hair styled without much effort, his blue sweater stretching across his broad chest, the edge of his white button down hanging over the waist of his jeans. "Need some help?" He motioned to the ornaments.

"Not until you tell me what you're doing here. You're about nine hundred miles south of New York."

Colin squatted down, picking an ornament from the box, letting the packing paper slip away. "I had a hankering for some Georgia barbecue." He studied her for a long hot moment, then cut a glance at the tree. "Is there any order to the ornament arrangement?"

"No." Bing was back with an old radio version of "Silent Night." Recorded right after the second war. *"It's a happy Christmas all right . . ."*

"Colin, you just hopped on a plane? And came down? For barbecue?"

Colin was silent for a beat. "Something like that." He raised a string of lights from the box. "What's this? Chili peppers?"

"And Mama's favorite. So handle with care." Avery reached for the strand. "She found them at the flea market. She and Daddy fought over buying them. 'Glo,' he said, 'those are not Christmas.' 'Yes they are, Gib. Look, red and green.'" Avery laughed softly. "Mama won, of course."

"Clearly." Colin grinned, pointing to the strand, rising up with a couple of ornaments in his hand. "How'd your interview go?" He glanced between Avery and the tree.

"Coach Boon seemed to like me for it. All that's left is the formalities." Avery retrieved a glass globe painted with a snowy, magical world. "Merry Christmas from Brighton." Susanna brought it home after Nathaniel's coronation.

After her relationship with Colin ended, Avery never cared much for the globe. It reminded her of too much. But tonight she set it on the checkout counter.

"Guess that makes you happy. Congratulations."

"I love the sport. And I need a career. So, yes, it makes me happy."

Colin picked a limb for one of his ornaments. "I always liked watching you play."

Avery frowned, peeking around at him. "What? W-when did you ever see me play?"

He shrugged, avoiding her gaze. "Y-you know. YouTube. ESPN. We have satellite that gets American sports channels." He cleared his throat, dropped his second ornament on a low branch, then dug in the box for another one . . . *waaay* in the bottom of the pile.

"Colin?" She leaned over him. "Y-you watched me play?"

He came up with an ornament, smoothing away the tissue paper. "A few times." He held up a water skiing reindeer, grinning. "I think this will be my favorite."

"Which times? When?" Now that he'd confessed, she wanted details.

"Tournaments. When you won the championship."

Avery turned away. All this time she'd believed he cared nothing for her. She whirled around to face him, chin raised. "Well?"

"Well what?"

"What did you think?"

He held her with his gaze, not letting go. "You were amazing. Very stellar."

"Avery—" Bristol burst in from the kitchen. "We're out." She gave Colin a good imitation of Mama's stink eye. "Unless you don't want to be alone with him. I can stay."

"I'm good, Bristol, thank you. I'll lock up the back. Do you have the deposit?"

She patted the bag tucked under her arm. "Right here. On my way to the bank right now."

"Have a good night."

"You too." Bristol angled toward Colin. "Behave yourself."

He stepped back, hands raised. "I'll be the perfect prince."

"Yeah? That's what I used to think about you, 'til you proved me wrong."

When she'd gone, Colin turned to Avery. "Guess I had that coming."

"Guess you did." Avery pushed past him for the kitchen. "Want a Coke or something?"

"Is it on the house?" He followed her, dusting his hands against his jeans, pausing with his gaze toward the stove. "Seems I should be greeting your father." He faced Avery. "Taking a hot biscuit from him."

"There're some fresh ones in that bin over there." Avery motioned to the prep table as she grabbed two glasses from a shelf and filled them with ice and Diet Coke.

Johnny Mathis crooned, *"I'll have a blue Christmas without you."*

But Colin passed, taking his glass from Avery, heading out to the deck.

Avery grabbed her hoodie from the hook by the door, then perched on the picnic table facing the ocean. She could hear its melody through the trees.

Colin slid in next to her and took a long sip of his soda.

"Why did you come, Colin? Really?" His end-of-day fragrance—soap mixed with his fading cologne—gentled over her senses. He always smelled so good.

"I wanted to see you." He started toward the trees. "I missed you. If that's allowed."

"I don't understand. Why? You're all but engaged to Lady Jordan."

"No, no, I'm not."

"Then why did you ring the bell? You had to know it would get people talking."

He sighed. "I didn't ring the bell, Avery."

"Then who did? Your friend, Guy? Wasn't he with you?"

"Guy didn't ring the bell either."

She bent forward to see his face. The flashing Christmas lights danced blue, green, and red across his august features. "Colin, what's going on?"

He raised his glass to his lips, looked sideways at her, a weary hope in his expression. "God rang the bell, Avery. At least I think it was Him."

Confession was good for the soul, but Avery's silence made him anxious. He slipped down from the picnic table, making his way to the edge of the deck.

He'd told her the whole story and now Avery had to process.

He knew from their brief but intense five-month relationship she required time to think.

"Want to walk?" he said, setting his glass on the table. "This weather is lovely, and it'd be a shame to come to St. Simons and not touch the beach."

"Sure." She hopped off the picnic table and headed down the path toward the Atlantic, where waves rushed the shore.

When they'd cleared the trees, the wind nipped down crisp and cold. Avery shivered, zipping up her thin hoodie.

"Here." Colin peeled off his sweater, offering it to her, extending his hand farther when she hesitated. "You need this more than I do."

"Are you sure?" But she took it from his fingers and slipped it over her head, wisps of her hair falling from a loose twist on the back of her head. "What will your dad say about you being here?"

"He doesn't know."

"Ah, still sneaking around at twenty-six?"

He laughed yet felt the subtle truth. "No. He's not privy to every detail of my private life."

They walked on in silence, their stride in rhythm with the wash of the waves. The path ahead was dark, though the moon cast a quarter of light over their shoulders. To the left, the amber orbs of street lamps beamed through the trees. In the distance a dog barked.

"Your board meeting?" she said. "How was it?"

"Boring enough. But we got the job done."

"And New York?"

"Crowded. Attempting Christmas cheer," he said.

"I like the city at Christmas, but there's no place like Cathedral City this time of year. Especially the ancient quarter with the narrow cobblestone streets, the shops so close, the thatched roofs, decorations everywhere, people in costume, caroling. Like how you dream Christmas should be."

"I like when the snow falls and the world is soft and quiet."

The shadows parted as they walked on, the light from the Rib Shack's deck growing smaller.

"Me too, but I love Christmas here, though," Avery said. "In the south. We have our traditions. Pecan pie, sweet potato pie, roasted oysters. Santa arriving on a speed boat." She ran her hands through her hair so more tendrils fell over her shoulder, tempting Colin to reach up and wind one curl about his finger. "For years, when I was a kid, Grandaddy had a fire pit going all day long. We'd go over midmorning after opening our presents and I'd run around with the cousins playing football in the meadow. They were all much older than me, but I worked hard to keep up. In the evening, Uncle Hud tuned up his banjo and plucked bluegrass Christmas carols. You haven't heard 'O Holy Night' until it's done with a twang. Then somewhere in the night I would fall asleep on Granny's floor under the lights of the Christmas tree." Her laugh echoed in the waves. "I sound like an old woman telling that story. Here I am, just twenty-two."

"It's a lovely memory."

"What about you? Any Christmas traditions you treasure?"

"The whole lot of it. The lights. The music. When I was a lad Dad started taking us to the symphony right before Christmas. Now it's a regular tradition with the royal family. Anyway, I was ten when I attended my first symphony and Dad bought me my first tuxedo. My sisters wore these poofy dresses that made lots of noise when they moved. Which was a lot during a two-hour performance. Mum shushed them so much she became a part of the music." He chuckled. "They were seven and five. Dad didn't take them again until they were much older."

"You really admire your dad, don't you?" Her tone communicated a revelation of some kind, a deeper understanding.

He tucked his hands into his pockets, hunched against the wind. "For all his faults, I do. He's my hero, really. The man I most admire. He was born with a silver spoon in his mouth, as they say, but he's worked hard to earn what he inherited. When Granddad retired, my father grew the company 50 percent in his first two years at the helm."

"So you have big shoes to fill."

"Very big." His step hit a dip in the sand and he stumbled, bumping into Avery. She raised a hand to steady him, her hand pressed against his chest, over his rumbling heart. He reached to hold on to her but she was too quick for him. "He's always believed in me. Almost to a fault, you see. He's the one person I cannot bear to disappoint."

Avery stopped walking, turning to him, her face accented with the jeweled glow of the moon. "Then why are you here? Is this a guilt trip? Look, I've moved on, Colin. Your dad made it clear I was not a good match for you."

"This is not a guilt trip, Avery. And my father does not determine my love life, despite what he might think. I just—"

"Just what, Colin? Why did you sneak down here?"

"I did not sneak."

"What reason will you give your father when he finds out and demands you never speak to me again?" She stepped into him, a raw boldness about her. "Listen, dude, my sister is going to have a baby and—"

"What? Are you serious? When? I never heard this."

She grimaced. "Ooo, sorry, yeah, the baby is still a secret. So don't say a word. But yes, she's pregnant and it's looking good."

He zipped his lips in a pledge of silence. "Your secret is safe with me. But how splendid. An heir. I'll say a prayer for this new prince or princess."

Avery's posture softened. "Th-thank you. That means a lot."

"Meanwhile, you were saying . . . my father will demand I never speak to you . . . but Susanna is having a baby so . . ."

"Just that I'll be visiting more. You can't ignore me." She sighed and turned, heading farther down the beach. "I don't know, maybe you can. You did a pretty good job of it the last few years."

"Avery." Colin caught her arm. "I'm sorry. Very sorry. But I did what I thought I had to do. Now I realize how painful it was and lacking in truth, integrity, and honor, all the things my father taught me—"

"But you were more than willing to forgo them all to get rid of me."

"Get rid of you? That's a gross mischaracterization. I never wanted to—"

"Gross mischaracterization?" She flipped her hand against the wind. "Not where I stand. The truth is you never *said* a thing."

"Granted, I should've been forthcoming. Told you the truth. But I was not trying to get rid of you." If he confessed she was the light of his life would she believe him? Probably not.

"Then you did an amazing imitation of it. What was it really? Besides distracting you from your studies. Besides not being Brightonian. I wasn't good enough, right?"

"What? Need I remind you your sister is married to our king. Don't be ridiculous . . . not good enough." Frustrated, he faced the water. They were talking in circles. But would telling her the rest of the story only complicate matters?

She came alongside him. "You know I loved you. I was ready to give up everything I'd dreamed of to marry you."

Colin enveloped her in his arms, cradling her head on his shoulder. "Darling, I loved you too. Very much."

She clung to him, her hands gripping his shirt, as her soft cry watered his heart. He rested his cheek against hers.

"I'm sorry, Avery. So very sorry."

They swayed together to the symphony of the ocean and the night sounds of the island. Her tears ebbed to a low shudder and her clutch on his shirt loosened. At last she stepped back, smoothing her hands over his chest.

"We should get back. I need a tissue and I left the Shack unlocked."

Colin slipped his hand into hers. "Do you forgive me, Avery? Please."

She nodded. "I did a long time ago. But you asking helps." She pulled her hand free and started back the way they came, the moon's low light creating a dim pathway. Then she stopped. "Wait. You said God rang the bell?"

He laughed. "That only took half an hour."

"Sorry, I was mulling it over, then we started talking about Christmas. So . . . what is this miracle you speak of?"

On their slow trek back, Colin recounted his annual tradition with Guy Smoot—of climbing the Pembroke bell tower with pipes and pints, talking over old times, over future times, and taking in the spectacular view of the city.

"This year Maddie and Hy raised awareness of the bell's history, of the last prince who rang the bell and then fell to his death.

So Guy asked me if I would ring the bell for Lady Jordan." The lights of the Rib Shack glowed brighter as they moved closer. "I said no, then spoke to God. I told Him if I were to ring the bell, it'd be for you." His confession came from the most secret place. And now it was out in the open, on the edge of the sea where the wind could take hold of it.

"You would ring the bell for me?"

"Yes, but you see, I didn't ring the bell. It rang on its own, and as I live and breathe, Avery, I know it was the hand of God."

"Why would He ring the bell?"

"I guess as some sort of answer to my prayer." Did he sound ridiculous? Why indeed would God ring the bell? "Do you think I'm making something out of nothing?"

She raised her hands, the sleeves of his sweater slipping down her arms. "Don't ask me. I'm out of the mix."

"But you're not, you see." He took hold of her. "You are the center of the mix. And I believe, yes, the reason the bell rang. I can't imagine any other explanation."

"Colin, it's my experience God leads with a still, small voice. And sometimes with giant miracles like Aurora popping out of the woods with a twenty-eight-hundred-dollar pair of shoes for Susanna. But this?"

"Avery, there was no wind that night. Even if there was, it would have to blow at a gale force to ring up a six-hundred-pound bell. The cord was still hooked to the wall, and all the while the bell was tolling over and over." He was convincing himself more than Avery. Which his soul needed.

"Okay, fine, God rang the bell. W-what are you saying? We're supposed to get married on Christmas Day?" She scoffed, starting again for the Rib Shack, her hair completely undone by the breeze and flapping behind her to the music of the waves. "I don't think so."

"Why not?"

She whirled around to face him. "Are you serious? We don't know each other anymore, Colin. And I'd never come between you and your dad. I don't know what you're thinking, but putting a wedge between you two is stupid. I won't be a part of it."

"Aren't you the one who challenged me? 'Still sneaking around at twenty-six?' I am my own man. I can make my choices and still be my father's son. You don't give him credit. He's a good man."

"Then call him right now. Tell him where you are." She waited for him to reach for his phone, then poked him in the chest. "You can't do it, can you? You can't deal with disappointing him."

Colin exhaled, his argument deflated. In all honesty, he didn't know if he could deal or not. He'd never pushed far enough past Dad's boundaries.

Avery started the path to the Shack deck but after a few steps turned back around. "For your information, Prince Colin, you broke my heart. That was the worst summer of my life. I had no idea a man could affect me the way you did. I fell hopelessly in love. At seventeen. I didn't want anything but you. College? Who cared? Volleyball? Wasn't my life goal anymore. Ohio State would survive without me. I wanted to be your wife, and the two of us would make a difference in the world. We'd have babies—"

"How many?"

"What?"

"I said how many?"

"I-I don't know . . . three?"

"Good, I was thinking three or four."

"Don't patronize me."

"I'm not. Go on. What else did you dream about this life we were to live?"

She tugged the sleeves of his sweater around her hands. "Well, we'd raise kids who loved Jesus and cared for people, who knew right from wrong, who had integrity. With your family's money and your place in the House of Stratton, we could've started foundations and charities. I envisioned a volleyball camp for underprivileged girls. Like Prince Stephen did with rugby, you know? I would live near my sister. We'd have family birthdays and holidays."

"Sounds perfect, love."

"Colin, stop. You don't get it. Nothing in my old world felt right after I met you, after you kissed me that night at Parrsons House. A part of my heart popped wide open. It took me years to shove it closed. Don't stand there being all charming and sweet, agreeing with my fantasy, when we both know nothing will ever come of it." Again, she turned to go but did a 360 to face him again. "You want to know the worst part?"

"Tell me." He submitted to her venting. To her truth-telling.

"I thought you felt the same way. Then—*Bam! Poof*—you're gone. Not just a little bit. A lot of bit. Fine, you couldn't make it to my high school prom. I was disappointed, but there's more to life than prom. But you never speaking to me again? You unfriended me on Facebook. You cut me off." She shook with the passion of her confession. "Until two weeks ago, I had no idea why. So don't come down here talking to me about God ringing a bell in answer to your little prayer. Because I prayed for four and a half years for you to call me, write me, reach out in some way, and all I got was the silent song. Now, I need to go lock up the Shack. You can stand here if you want but I'm leaving."

"Avery, wait." Colin's heart swelled with the rest of the truth. The secret only Dad knew. "I was going to propose." There. He'd confessed. The truth was all the way out. "That's the rock-bottom reason why Dad did not want me to come, Avery. I was going to ask you to marry me."

CHAPTER 14

W hat did you just say?" The waves thundered and a ghostly glow broke through a thin strata of clouds.

"I think you heard me, Avery. I was going to propose. I'd taken my grandmother's ring from the family vault."

"You were going to propose . . . marriage? To me?"

"Yes."

She faced away from him, trying to comprehend. Trying to feel something besides bewilderment. "Your dad found out?"

"The bank manager saw me go into the vault. He alerted Dad."

"Your father really doesn't care for me, does he?"

"It's not you, Avery. It's more your American heritage. He's a patriot. Which I believe you can appreciate. He wants a Brighton girl for me. He also thought I was, we were, too young. I had a lot of schooling and training ahead of me. As did you."

"Why can't young people know if they have found their true love? No one asked me what I thought of marrying you. I was robbed."

"How was I to do that? 'Hello, love. I was thinking of proposing, but Dad says we're too young and have too much work ahead of us. What do you think?' How would you have answered?"

"Yes. I would've answered 'Yes, I'll marry you.' I'd have stood by you in your training. I'd have gone to school in Brighton." The words she'd bottled up flowed, free from their deep confinement. "We weren't too young. I didn't want to party with friends or date other men. I'd found you. Where was I to go from there?"

Raw and real, her confession revealed how much she'd loved him. Too late to regret her honesty.

Colin cleared his throat. "W-what if I proposed now?"

"Ha!" She walked up the path to the Shack's back deck. "Now you're being cruel."

He caught up to her. "No, I mean it. What if the bell was God pointing me toward you? What if now is our time?"

She reached for the screen door, moving into the lit and warm kitchen. From the dining room, the jukebox played "Have a Holly Jolly Christmas."

"Go home, Colin. The hardest thing I ever had to do was get over you. I don't want to do that again."

"You think it was easy for me?"

"Sure looked easy from where I sat, bubba." Walking through the kitchen, she checked to make sure everything was powered down and flipped off the lights. Heading into the dining room, she glanced back at Colin. "You can go. I'm going to finish decorating. Where are you staying?" That's it . . . keep the conversation shallow. On surface details.

"At Nathaniel's cottage."

Ah, the cottage. Where her sister fell in love with the prince-turned-king while designing his garden.

"Guess I'll see you in Brighton." She turned to the tree, the limbs blurring together as her tears started to rise. "When do you go back?"

"Tomorrow."

She nodded. "I leave Friday."

"Avery, we need to talk about what I just said. You can't just ignore my words."

She turned to him. "Sure I can. I feel myself being drawn back to you and I'm sorry, I can't. I won't. I don't care about ringing bells or what you prayed to the Lord. That's for you to figure out. Here's a tip. If you really want to marry a girl, ring the bell yourself. Then she'll be confident you love her. But for now, let's just go our separate ways." She gave him her best, I'm-good-with-this smile.

"I'll go, but this conversation is not over." He collected his coat and bid her good night, then paused at the door. "For what it's worth, getting over you was the hardest thing I ever had to do in my life. Naval training was easy in comparison." He exhaled. "In fact, Avery, I'm not sure I am over you at all."

"Take that back." She hurried after him, shoving the door closed, and twisting the lock. "That's not fair, Colin. Not fair. And I don't believe you." She hammered the door with her fist as Blake Shelton's Christmas version of "Home" drifted through the restaurant. "Take it back." Avery kicked the door, then gradually slipped down to the floor, sobbing, dropping her forehead against the soft, fragrant wool of Colin's sweater.

CHAPTER 15

December 16
Nine days until Christmas

Madeline & Hyacinth Live! Show

Madeline: "Hyacinth, the prince is
in New York this week."
Madeline: "You think he's running? Hiding?"
Hyacinth: "Maybe he's gone off to look
for a male and female goat."
Madeline: (Laughing) "In New York? Goats of
the cashmere kind . . . already made into
jackets and sweaters. He does have that
lovely navy blue cashmere coat I love."
Hyacinth: (Waving about a set of blue cards)
"Maddie, do you think he's changed his
mind? I'm afraid he's changed his mind."

Madeline: "Hy, we don't know if he actually made *up* his mind. All we know is he came running out of the tower with the bell tolling to kingdom come."

Hyacinth: "Meanwhile, Lady Jordan is in London in talks for a new film. (shaking her head) I'm not hopeful here. This is killing me."

Colin muted the volume of his office telly and pushed away from his desk, stretching and pouring another cup of coffee from the service cart by the door.

Poor Hyacinth. She was going to be really disappointed Christmas Day when there was no wedding at Watchman Abbey.

Sipping his coffee, he made his way back to his desk. Exhausted and bleary-eyed, Colin determined to finish his report on the board meeting. Procrastination had no place at Tattersall Ltd. Especially as the grandson of the founder and son of the CEO.

He'd left Jacksonville late Thursday afternoon for New York. Then picked up his flight to Cathedral City. He tried to catch forty winks while crossing the Atlantic, but he grappled with the reality of God actually ringing the bell, of telling Avery the truth.

The haunting tone of her *"Take that back"* lived in his heart.

Work. He needed to work. Get focused on his life. His future. He'd been mad to fly down to St. Simons. Looney to confess the truth.

He'd come to the office straight from the airport, asked the office admin for a pot of coffee, and got to work. He'd have this report down before end of business. Indeed.

Meanwhile, for background noise, he flipped on the *Madeline & Hyacinth Live!* show, hoping the buzz about his supposed bell ringing had died.

Nope.

He worked for a few minutes but weariness hindered his concentration and allowed thoughts of Avery to remain in residence.

Moving to the window by his desk, Colin gazed down to the street below where a shower of snowflakes turned the world magical and white. Afternoon shoppers hurried down the sidewalk, their arms laden with bags and boxes.

Across the way, oh about two miles, was his loft apartment. He had a skyline view of the city from there too. But the place was bare and cold, only a bed and dresser in his bedroom, a chair and telly in the living area. He didn't care to reside there much, preferring the hubbub and coziness of home. Of his sisters chatting over the chaps at uni. Mum and Dad discussing the social calendar.

Mum tried to set up a decorator for his flat but Colin canceled every time. He had a chair for sitting to watch the telly. A bed for sleeping and a spoon and bowl for his morning cereal. What else did a bachelor need?

A lovely bride to make his cold space warm.

"Lord, what are You asking of me?"

He'd known the touch of the Divine. Especially out at sea. One particular storm, even the captain urged the crew to pray.

But the supernatural bell ringing was new territory for him. The question was, could he figure out the message and obey? Avery's admonition to ring the bell himself if he loved a woman hit a cord. Was he being a coward, hiding behind God? Yet, if Colin was going to buck his dad, he'd need the help of heaven. Avery nailed that point as well.

Colin remained at the window, waiting, listening. To his left Cathedral City's ancient stone streets wove between narrow buildings, then spilled out to a twenty-first-century speedway.

The sidewalks were peppered with dark-suited businessmen and women hustling through the cold and past the flashing Christmas lights for a Friday evening at their favorite pub.

He'd been one of those pub hustlers his first six months at the firm. But after a while he found it vain and empty. He'd rather spend the evening with true friends, with his family.

"Colin?" Dad entered without knocking. "Julian ran the expenses from your trip." He kept a tight rein on the company accounting. "What's this?" He floated a printout of his corporate credit card records onto the desk.

The ticket to Jacksonville. He didn't even have to look. "I'll pay for it, Dad."

"Of course you will. But I'm not concerned about the money. I'm concerned why you took the flight in the first place. New York to Jacksonville? You went to see her, didn't you? I spoke to Nathaniel. He told me she went home for some sort of interview."

"So you're checking up on me now?" Colin returned to his desk, setting his coffee cup on a Knoxton University coaster.

"Not until I saw this."

"So you went to Nathaniel instead of me."

Dad's expression darkened. "It was incidental. I had tea with him this week. He told me his sister-in-law—"

"Avery."

"Yes, Avery went to America for a job opportunity."

"Looks like she has a coaching job," Colin said. "So no need to fear I'll chase after her. What would I do with myself in America?"

"Then why did you bother with the time and expense to see her when she'll be here all season? Colin, don't stir up the past. What good can come of it?"

"She needed to know the rest of the story. Why I let her down."

"The rest of the story? Son, you didn't tell her—"

"I did."

Dad's cheeks flushed red and his sharp gaze narrowed. "I can't see the wisdom in that, Colin. Why on earth would you do such a thing?"

"She needed to know why I cut off all communication. 'I was busy,' or 'Schooling consumed me' just did not suffice, Dad. I'm sorry, but I had to tell her."

Dad shook his head. "Then be prepared for whatever consequences come."

Colin slowly pushed to his feet, feeling the weariness of his journey. "Dad, you know I respect you. You're the first one I seek out when I need counsel, but you can't manage every moment of my life. You can't expect me to respond to life the way you do. I went to St. Simons to see a friend and I don't deserve a dressing down from you."

His heart pulsed as he waited for Dad's reaction.

He sighed, pacing, tapping his hand against his leg. "In matters of the heart, I worry."

"Well, stop. This is my journey. Granddad didn't hover over you. I'm my own man, and if you don't trust how I turned out, then you and Mum need to sort it out. I'm twenty-six, not six."

"We trust how you turned out. And Granddad didn't hover over me because I was even more driven than he. But you?" Dad reached for the accounting printout. "You've a tender side. I didn't see it in you until you met Avery. I admire you for it. Yet I fear it will trip you up. You are in a rare position with one foot in the royal world and one in business. Your bloodline goes all the way back to King Stephen I on my side as well as your mother's. You are a prince for the people. Even that silly cupcake business proved my point. You are the bridge between the common man and the royal one."

"So you've said. Many times. If you must know, Avery's gone off me. She knows you disapprove and won't come between us."

"Really?" Dad moved toward the door, his expression contemplative. "Then I underestimated her."

"I'd say you have."

"I'll be more cordial . . . Ah, when I see her at the symphony tomorrow." He smiled. "She'll be there?"

"I suppose."

"And you're still on to bring Lady Jordan?"

"Not sure. We've not spoken—" As if she had some cosmic bug in Colin's office, Lady Jordan lit up his phone. "Speaking of . . ." He answered and Dad made his exit. "Jordan."

"Love, I've missed you. I thought you'd ring by now . . . about tomorrow."

"Sorry, I was away on business." Why bother to mention she'd never rang him after his voice message. "Will you be ready at seven? I'll come round with the car."

"Lovely. Looking forward to it. I'll be in a hot red dress."

Colin hung up, tossing his phone aside. He bet she'd be in a hot red dress. Not one to squander a media moment, Lady Jay would bring the full Monty.

He'd have found her comment amusing before the Harvest Celebration. Now he was annoyed. Not with her, to be fair, but with himself. Once a man found a better way, it made no sense to carry on as he did before. His appetites and longings changed.

Colin sat at his desk, a gnawing sensation growing in his belly. His life course had been altered. He just had to figure out where to go from here.

CHAPTER 16

December 17
Eight days before Christmas

"Avery Mae." Mama barged into her suite, her black-and-white gown flowing about her, a soft pink cashmere shrug about her shoulders. She wore makeup and her silver hair was coiled on top of her head.

Avery exited her room, phone and the clutch Susanna lent her in hand, wearing the gown she wore to Nathaniel's coronation ball. She was bone-tired. Happy about her job prospects. Yet unsettled over her conversation with Colin.

He was truly going to propose? What was she to do with that four and a half years later?

She had arrived in Cathedral City late last night only to be rousted out of bed early by Susanna. They had an eight a.m. appointment with the designer, Ferny, who was designing an extraordinary Christmas Ball gown.

She used a white spun wool so fine it felt like silk and a satin blend. The skirt flowed from the bodice in overlapping layers that clung to Avery's lean frame all the while flowing free. Avery had never seen anything like it.

The fitted bodice was of the same fabric with faux fur added to the cap sleeves. The hem was edged in a royal blue. When she tried it on she felt instantly at peace.

The only thing she didn't like? It was white. Looked way too much like a wedding dress. Worse, it felt like a wedding dress. Which haunted her in the aftermath of her conversation with Colin. A conversation she decided to keep to herself. At least for now.

In the sitting room of her suite, she whistled at Mama. "Look at you. Are you giving Queen Campbell a run for her money?"

Tonight was the Royal Brighton Symphonic presenting "An Evening of Carols." An event Avery had been dying to attend since Susanna got married.

"Ha, hardly. Queen Campbell is her own shining star." Mama pointed to Avery's phone, arching her brow. "What I want to know is why you're hauling that with us to the symphony?"

"I haul it everywhere."

"Ain't nothing important going to come through on a Saturday night. Put that thing away. You're off for an evening of Christmas with the symphony." Mama lowered her voice as she patted her hand against her updo. This was not the Glo Truitt Avery grew up with.

"I can check my e-mail during intermission. I want to hear the carols too. But if Coach Boon e-mails—"

"You were just there this past week. He's not going to e-mail you on a Saturday night." Mama took Avery's phone from her hand.

"You need to unplug and relax. Look at me. Being away from the Rib Shack has done me a world of good."

"I know. It's actually scaring me a little." Avery pinched back her phone away from her mama. "I'll put it on vibrate. But this thing is going with me."

Mama regarded her for a moment. "So, everything was good at the Shack?"

"Running like clockwork." Avery tucked her phone into her clutch and started for the door. "Ready?"

"Hold on." Mama gave her the Glo-stare. The one that could get the innocent to confess a crime they didn't commit. "Is everything all right? Anything happen back home I need to know about?"

"Not really. I had to decorate the Shack for Christmas." Avery shrugged. "That was unexpected but fun."

"That ain't no big deal." Mama waved off Avery's comment, narrowing her truth-pulling gaze. "Are you sure ain't nothing bothering you?"

"Yes, ma'am. Now can we go?"

Photographers swarmed Royal Leopold Hall, colored spotlights flashing from the ground, patrons and ticket holders filing into the foyer as the limo with the king's party pulled around.

Protection officers held a protective line as Nathaniel stepped out first, aiding Susanna, then the queen, followed by Mama. The last to exit, Avery slid over to the door, reaching for her brother-in-law's hand.

But when she stepped out, it wasn't Nathaniel holding on to her but Prince Colin.

"Hello." Aware her hand remained in his, she walked with him through the doors into the royal-blue-and-gold carpeted foyer.

"How are you?" He helped her from her coat, offering it to the porters who worked the coatroom, his presence taking her back to the first night they met. He'd been so attentive and sweet, introducing her to his high-brow, aristocratic friends in a manner that made her feel accepted. Wanted.

She took a step back, gripping her beaded clutch in her hands. "I'm good."

"So we meet again," Lady Jordan interrupted, bumping past Colin to shake Avery's hand.

"Yes, we meet again." The warmth she sensed from Colin faded in the wake of Jordan's cool beauty.

"Colin, darling, there's Bobo Lyle. Let me go schmooze." And Jordan was off, waving at someone across the room.

"Is she like, what, your date to all official functions?" Avery said.

"We made this date before the Harvest Celebration." Colin closed the space between them. "She's just a friend."

"With whom you have a romantic relationship?"

"No." He tugged at his white, stiff collar. "We were semi-romantic at one time but—"

"Semi-romantic?" Avery made a face. "I'm not sure I know what that means."

"Aves." Susanna tapped her arm. "We're going in. Colin, are you sitting with us or your parents? Princess Rachel and Prince Anthony aren't here. You can have their seats."

"Thank you, Susanna."

Avery exhaled. What did Colin want from her? Why was he . . . flirting . . . when they both knew nothing could come of their relationship? And he was here with Jordan, for crying out loud.

In the royal box, Avery felt his presence. And Jordan's. She checked her phone one more time, desperate for an e-mail from Coach Boon, then hopped over to Facebook and saw Colin had sent her a Friend request. She peered at him, then hit Delete.

She'd go home soon and start her life. She didn't need memories of him floating up whenever she saw his posts on Facebook.

"Aves," Mama hissed. "Put that thing away."

Avery frowned, tucking her phone back into her clutch, then secured it beside her in her seat. *See, Mama?*

Then the music started, parting her heart, sowing seeds of hope. Closing her eyes, Avery sang with the song of the violins and cellos.

"O holy night . . ."

The glorious sounds of Christmas filled the hall. Song after song. A choir robed in red and gold lined up in the aisle proclaiming *"Glory to the newborn king."*

The orchestra crescendoed with bass drums. A swirl of joy swept across her bones. Avery rubbed the shivers from her arms. This was what her soul needed.

The stage went dark and the house lights rose. Intermission. The audience stood, stretching, the din of their voices replacing the violins, cellos, and flutes as they made their way to the foyer.

Avery reached for her clutch, glancing over at Colin, who was fixed on the program, reading with a pair of dark glasses.

"Look at you, all smart looking with those specs."

He looked up. "Do I look smart?"

"You do." She slipped her phone from her clutch. It was a habit more than a need. "You should wear them more often."

"Very funny."

Susanna passed Avery a water bottle as she took a peek at her e-mail. She couldn't put her finger on it, but she had a feeling Coach Boon would e-mail her this weekend.

Her hands flashed cold when she saw Boon's name in the new e-mail downloads, subject line, "Your Visit."

Angling forward she read his message.

It was a pleasure to meet you, Avery. You are the kind of girl and player a coach needs on this team. However—

She drew in a sharp breath. Susanna glanced around. "What is it?"

—we've decided to go another way. I wish you all the best on your endeavors.

Avery flipped over her phone, shaking, glancing toward the exit, tears blurring her vision. They didn't want her.

"Excuse me," she said as she fumbled from the royal box, passing under the swags of garland, and fleeing through the narrow private hall and down the stairs to the outside.

He watched her go. Something she read on her phone had upset her. Colin whispered toward Lady Jordan, "I'll be right back."

He slipped through the box and the murmur of voices, down the hall after her, catching the ends of Avery's burnished curls as she burst through the door to the outside.

"Avery, what's wrong?"

She shivered, her face toward the night sky as a fresh snow began to fall. "It's stupid. I don't know why it's upsetting me so much."

"Here . . ." He shimmied from his tuxedo jacket and draped it over her shoulders.

She glanced at her phone, then shook it at Colin. "This stupid phone. I-I can't make a call."

"You want to make a call now?" He tucked his hands into his pockets, hunching against the cold. Tuxedo shirts aren't very thick.

"They don't want me."

"Who doesn't . . . Ah, that coaching job."

She sighed, slapping the phone against her leg. "They decided to go another way, whatever that means." She flicked a tear from the corner of her eye. "But I have to call him. See why he turned me down."

From the west wing of the hall, photographers roamed, coming in from the shadows.

Colin ignored them but turned away, hiding his face. "You can't take this personally, Avery. There's no telling what factored into their decision. I've seen this at our firm several times. We have a stellar candidate, then one comes along who has something extra that puts him or her in first place. Like one had negotiating experience. It put him over the equally qualified candidate who did not."

"I need to know, Colin. I won't be able to sleep. My whole future was riding on this."

"Here, give me your phone." Colin's fingers brushed hers. She was cold and trembling. "Do you want to go inside?"

"No. The cold feels good."

"What's his name and number?"

"Coach Boon. I don't know his number. It's in my contacts."

"All right. Look at me, I'm your secretary." He tapped on her phone, searching the contacts. When he found Coach Boon, he motioned for her to retrieve his phone from his breast pocket. "Love, hand me my phone."

Using his phone, he dialed the coach's number, then slipped his arm around Avery as he put his phone on speaker.

"How'd you do that?" Avery whispered when the first ring sounded.

"I make a lot of international calls." Colin jerked to attention when a deep voice answered with a Southern hello.

"Yes, Coach Boon?"

"Speaking."

"This is Prince Colin of Brighton Kingdom. Could you hold for Avery Truitt? She'd like a word."

"Um, all right? Who is this again?"

Avery covered her mouth as Colin offered his phone. "Well?"

She hesitated, then took the phone off speaker, pressing it to her ear. "Coach, hey, this is Avery Truitt . . . Yes, that was Prince Colin . . . Really. Look, I'm sorry to bother you but I just got your e-mail and . . ." She exhaled sending an array of pale crystals swirling in front of her. "I'm confused . . ." She listened for half a minute, her eyes fixed on the falling snow. "I see . . . Well, yes, I understand. Thank you for taking the time to talk to me."

She lowered the phone, peering at Colin. "A former Valdosta player interviewed last minute for the job. She knew the program. They gave it to her." She forced a smile. "Guess there's something else out there for me."

"I'm so sorry, Avery. Don't get discouraged."

"Did you ever lose a job? Or not get hired?"

"No."

"That's not part of your world, is it?"

"Doesn't mean my world is easy, love. My world is highly defined and contained with a lot of expectations. Before I was born, my destiny was set for me."

"That sounds pretty nice right now."

"Come, let's go back inside. I'll buy you a hot chocolate. And I know the way up to the rafters." He held up his hand. "Don't ask me how. We can watch the symphony from there."

"Won't Lady Jordan miss you?"

"Fifty quid she's sitting with Bobo Lyle or some other stepping-stone in her career." He winked, took her hand, and led her inside into the mournful melody of "O Come O Come Emanuel."

Avery stopped, her hand still in his. "Wait. This was one of Daddy's favorite songs."

"Then let's stand here and listen."

"Rejoice, rejoice, Emanuel . . ."

Avery rested her head on his shoulder. "Thank you, Colin. I mean it."

December 19
Six days until Christmas

Madeline & Hyacinth Live! Show

Madeline: "Well, Hy, the symphony
was lovely Saturday night."

Hyacinth: "Perfectly spectacular. And, to my delight,
Prince Colin was there with Lady Jordan."

Madeline: "But we still have no
   formal announcement!"

Hyacinth: "I've decided they want to surprise us."

Madeline: "Best brace yourself, Hy. Our spies around
   Cathedral City have not seen one goat traversing
   toward Lady Jordan's place at Cannington Park."

Hyacinth: "Of course not. She lives
   in luxury apartments."

Madeline: (Shaking her head) "I know you really
   wanted a royal Christmas wedding at the
   abbey, with the elegant Lady Jordan swooning
   over the handsome Prince Colin but—"

Hyacinth: "As did you, Maddie. Hang on, love,
   we've six more days. You never know."

Madeline: "Your eternal optimism annoys me.
   But curiosity got the better of me over
   the weekend and I called on my contacts
   with the top designers in town and not
   one bit of a hint that they are designing
   some luxurious wedding gown."

Hyacinth: "Well, of course they're not going to
   tell you. We're two of the loudest mouths in
   Brighton Kingdom. We'd never keep it a secret
   and they know it. (Hyacinth made a face for
   the camera.) Stay tuned for more. We'll be
   right back with boy band Meant to Be Mine,
   singing Christmas carols and talking about
   their latest album, already gone platinum."

CHAPTER 17

December 19
Six days until Christmas

Colin paced outside his cousin's office, whose secretary, Olivia, eyed him over the rim of her glasses. This morning he woke with the urge for counsel. Though this time, not from his father but his cousin and king.

So he popped round to his office unannounced. He'd waited almost an hour to speak to him. But he wasn't leaving. He must speak to Nathaniel. Otherwise he'd burst.

Olivia brought him a cup of tea and a plate of biscuits. "Why did you ring the Pembroke Chapel bell?"

How long had she been waiting to ask that one? "It's complicated."

"Isn't love always complicated?" She smirked and sashayed back to her desk.

"Isn't Nathaniel available yet?" Colin sipped his tea, peering toward the king's office.

"His Majesty has a very full diary, but I'll get you in for a few moments."

"Th-thank you." He smiled for Olivia. It behooved him to be kind to the mistress of the king's diary or he'd find himself waiting away most of the day.

He'd just taken a seat, willing his bones to relax, when Nathaniel's door opened. "Cousin Colin, come in. What a nice surprise. Olivia, no calls, please."

"Yes, sir," Olivia said.

Balancing his tea and biscuits, Colin made his way into Nathaniel's office. He'd played in here a few times as a lad, when Dad visited Uncle Leo. Dad always made a point of bringing Colin with him when he met with important men.

"What's on your mind?" Instead of sitting, Nathaniel reached for his coat and scarf. "Leave your coat on, Colin. Come with me."

"Where to?" He set his cup and saucer on the tea cart and followed his cousin through a private door to a narrow passageway and secret staircase.

"I need to stretch my legs," Nathaniel said. "The morning has been tense with one meeting after another, and arrangements for the state dinner in the new year." He glanced back at Colin. "Susanna wants to have the whole family over on New Year's Eve. We'll welcome in the year and say good-bye to Glo and Avery. They leave on the second. Shall I count you in? You'll be all right round Avery?"

"I love her." The words rocketed from Colin without any explanation and echoed in the narrow space along with the tapping of their footsteps against the marble stairs. "I don't want to, but I do."

"You love her?" Nathaniel, ever so calm and rather irritating about it, exited a tall, hand-carved door into a private court. "Are we talking about Avery?"

"Of course Avery. You think I'd be here if it were Lady Jordan?" Colin pulled his gloves from his coat pocket. The wind was sharp today. "I'm sorry, Nathaniel. I don't mean to be rude."

"No need. You forget I've been where you are, under the spell of a Truitt girl."

Overhead, the December sky hosted a glorious sun in a sea of blue. Low stratus clouds stacked toward the horizon, like waves rolling toward the shore.

"I see Susanna's been here," Colin said, surveying the winter garden of green firs and red-leaf plants that thrived in Brighton's cold.

"Gardening runs in her veins." Nathaniel pulled on his gloves. "I had to give her the interior courtyards to work or risk mutiny with the garden yeoman. She changes this one for every season."

Colin grinned. "Some of the yeomen's families have worked the royal gardens for generations."

"Brightonians love their tradition. To our detriment sometimes."

"You're referring to the bell now, aren't you?"

"Madeline and Hyacinth seem to be having a jolly time with it." He started down the walk, toward a wrought iron gate. "They'll be so disappointed if there's no Christmas Day wedding."

"Surely in all of Brighton, someone is marrying on Christmas."

"Not a prince. Not at Watchman Abbey."

Leaving the garden, the king and his cousin walked over snow-covered grounds, down a small slope toward the trees, away from the public's prying eye.

"What do I do?" No other context was needed.

"What any man does when he's in love. He pursues her or moves on."

"I moved on. Or so I'd thought. But now that I've seen her, talked to her, I-I can't get her out of my head."

"Did you ring the bell?"

Snow crunched under their feet. Winter birds flitted from bare limb to bare limb with a song in their throats.

"You promise not to think I'm mad if I tell you the truth?"

"Oh, I don't know, mate." Nathaniel laughed. "I've always thought you were a bit daft."

"All right, all right, big cousin," Colin said with a laugh, then sobered. "I didn't ring the bell."

"Then who did? Guy Smoot? Surely not? Then he'd have to swallow his pride and marry Lady Sarah."

"He'd choke and kill himself." Colin's foot slipped on the downslope of the hill, but he caught himself. "You didn't hear it from me, but he loves her."

"As I suspected." Nathaniel treaded on, hands in his coat pocket, his shoulders back, head high.

"The bell rang on its own."

Nathaniel stopped, turning to Colin. "Impossible. That bell weighs—"

"Six hundred pounds. I know. But I'm telling you, it rang on its own."

Nathaniel started toward the trees. "Then tell me why the bell rang on its own."

"That's the mad part . . . You see, I told God I'd ring the bell . . . if I could marry Avery. Then out of nowhere, the blame thing started ringing up. Far better than I could've done, I'll tell you."

"Ah." Nathaniel cut a kingly grin. "God rang the bell."

"Yes, or so it seems. There was no wind. No other man aboard but Guy. The bell cord remained hooked to the wall."

"You prayed and God answered. What's your dilemma?"

Nathaniel. So pragmatic. "How can I know for sure? Why would God do such a thing?"

"If you want details, ask Him. But I dare say He was breaking into your world, answering your prayer. 'Yes, if you ring the bell you should marry Avery. In fact, lad, I'll ring it for you.'"

"But how can I be sure? Would the God of the universe truly have time to lean over heaven to answer a chap like me with his faithless prayer?"

"The fact that you uttered a prayer in His name speaks of your faith, even if weak. He answered you in such a dynamic way to assuage your doubts."

"Then what do you advise concerning—"

"Your father?"

"He won't be for this. In fact, he may well fight against it."

"You're right to honor him. But, Colin, when he asked you to end the relationship the first time, he was a voice of reason."

"True. I was going to propose, Nathaniel. At your home on St. Simons. In the garden."

Nathaniel's smile neither agreed nor condemned. "Now I see why Edward was so adamant."

"He's never steered me wrong, Nathaniel. He's fought for me and my future since before I was born. I feel like I owe him."

"Have you shared any of this with Avery?"

"Not sure there was wisdom in doing so, but yes, I told her. She insists she won't come between me and Dad. She's not so keen on me, really. Said getting over me was the hardest thing she ever had to do."

"It was, Colin. She really loved you." Spoken like a brother-in-law, not a king or cousin. He quickened his pace as he walked through a stand of trees,

"I don't know what to do, Nathaniel." Colin unbuttoned his coat, warm with exercise. "I love her, but it feels rather selfish. If I pursue her, I alienate my father." Colin held up his hand. "If I side with Dad, I lose Avery. I can't bear it, I cannot. Yet all that aside, what of her career? Her desire to coach? She was most upset about losing the job in Georgia."

"Here's the challenge." Nathaniel stopped short, facing Colin. "Are you willing to obey your heavenly Father, who so graciously made Himself known to you, or succumb to fear and the will of your earthly father? Have you considered God might be working in your dad as well?"

Colin sighed, the truth of Nathaniel's words hitting dead center.

"At what point does God get to speak to you God-to-man? At what point does He become your Father? In the eyes of the law and society you're a man. You owe your father respect, make no mistake. You seek his counsel. But you're on your own journey now, Colin. Not your father's. God just might want to direct you in a way Edward wouldn't agree with or understand."

"Blimey, Nathaniel, you got all of that from the bell ringing on its own?"

Nathaniel's chuckle was kind. "I never believed in signs until I met Susanna. The bell was a sign, an invitation into God's heart. It doesn't mean run off and do what you want. It means talk to Him. 'Do I marry Avery Truitt?' He'll answer you."

"Not by Christmas, I'm guessing."

"You never know, cousin. Have faith."

"I have no guarantee Avery will give me a chance."

The air was so still. As if listening. Hard to imagine that on the other side of the bordering trees was the hustle and bustle of a metropolitan city.

"Colin, I walked into parliament with the first Order of Council from a monarch in a hundred years, asking them to change the marriage law for me, risking my reputation as a young king, without any assurance Susanna would accept me."

"You knew she loved you, surely." Colin had been a part of Nathaniel's proposal scheme. Along with Avery. It was one of his favorite memories.

"Susanna told me face-to-face she'd not marry me. Much in the same way Avery's told you. She'd not come between a king and his country. But I had to try. Otherwise I'd regret it. I had the Marriage Act to challenge. You have your father." Nathaniel motioned toward the palace. "I had to choose between God and my royal responsibility, between my heart and the law. You have to choose between God and your father. I feared the parliament the same way you fear Edward." He glanced at his watch. "We best get back."

Colin fell in step with his cousin, Nathaniel's counsel resonating in him. "Was it the best thing you ever did? Marrying Susanna?"

The king's smile spoke a thousand words. "So much so I can't imagine who I would be without her. She brought life to the family, to the kingdom. If it wasn't for her influence, I'm not sure the Duchess of Hessenberg would've accepted her role as the long lost princess. What a difference that made for the Grand Duchy. Look at my brother, Stephen. What a different chap he's become because he married the woman he loved. Love is a powerful force."

"Dad thinks it a disgrace Brighton's first family married foreigners."

"I'm sorry he feels so, but I'd not have it any other way. I'd have married a Brighton woman if I'd fallen in love with one. Are you in love with Lady Jordan?"

Colin shook his head.

"Then why pretend?"

"So the kingdom wouldn't mind another American in the royal family?"

"Colin, if God chooses once again to infuse our family with the DNA of an American, we will graciously embrace her. All the more if it's Avery Truitt." He grinned with another fast glance at his watch, leading the way up the slope toward the garden gate. "I really do need to get on. I'm meeting some old mates for lunch."

"I hardly hear you talk of your old friends anymore."

"Susanna reminds me I'm a man who needs friends. Being a king is what I do, not who I am. She said, 'Hang out with your bros.'"

"Bros? She really said bros?"

"She really said bros."

Saying good-bye at the private stairs, Colin exited a side door, making his way toward his car, thoughts spinning, his love for Avery Truitt in full bloom again.

She played Christmas tunes from her laptop as she sat on the floor of her suite, papers spread around, figuring out her next career move.

She'd printed out the name of every volleyball coach on the eastern seaboard, those she knew, those she didn't. Men and women with the best reputations.

Her first call went to her Ohio State coach. "Avery, I'd love to hire you, but we don't have any openings. How are things since your father died?"

Avery briefed her coach on life since graduation, but she wasn't down with chitchat. She wanted a job.

"What if I volunteered? Came on my own dime?"

"I'd love it. CJ Vogt is shaping up to be an outside hitter of your caliber. But are you sure you want to do that?"

"I'll be there. Right after Christmas."

He offered to give her names of other coaches who might be looking, which she eagerly accepted. But if a job didn't open up, her plan was to volunteer at her alma mater. Daddy left her a little bit of money. She could live cheap for a while. Bunk with friends still in Columbus.

She could waitress too. If she knew anything as much as volleyball it was how to work a restaurant.

Exhausted, she flopped back onto the floor, covering her eyes with her arm.

She hated waiting. Folks who waited got left behind and left out. Avery was a doer. Besides, she'd heard more than her share of woulda-shoulda-coulda stories from the old boys who sat on the Shack deck Monday afternoons, talking about the good old days. How they could've all been pro football stars if they'd only . . .

Worse, it was six days until Christmas and the joy of the season remained a stranger. She'd hoped her Brighton Christmas would be magical and romantic.

She'd not done a lick of shopping. This afternoon. For sure. She'd hit Glidens and Martings, and the shops on Market Avenue, then take a dreamy walk among the shops of Old Towne where

Christmastime truly became old world with horse-drawn carriages and sleigh bells ringing in the air.

Pushing off the floor, she moved to the window, where the day passed by lovely and blue. Her inner turmoil was over her job situation, right? Nothing to do with Prince Colin.

He wasn't in church yesterday so Avery had not seen him since the symphony debacle. He'd been so kind and sweet. A rock of confidence.

They sat in the rafters listening to the music, his shoulder lightly brushing hers, saying nothing, saying everything.

Avery pressed her forehead to the window. "I love him. There, I said it. Lord, I love him."

I am the Way.

The phrase rattled her comfort zone of worry.

I am the Way.

"I don't understand." She paced the suite and rested her hands in her hip pockets. She'd had this kind of God moment before, though few and far between. The last time she'd been facedown on her bedroom carpet crying over the same boy she'd just declared she loved.

He whispered the same words then. *I am the Way.*

A knock resonated on her door and Susanna peeked inside, grinning. She was dressed in a dark-green tweed suit with a matching hat.

"You look pretty."

"The National Gardner Association Christmas Tea is this afternoon." She hovered by the door. "There's someone to see you."

"Me?"

Susanna wiggled her eyebrows. "Yes, you. Come on."

Avery smoothed her hands down her jeans, then over her hair. "Who is it?"

"You'll see."

Avery tugged on her boots, then pulled the tie from her hair, letting out her ponytail, and followed Susanna downstairs, her heartbeat curious.

Was it Colin? Who else would have Susanna so excited? Was Avery ready to see him? Yes, no, wait.

"Suz, is it Colin?" Avery pinched her cheeks, drawing color to her pale cheeks.

In the library off the foyer, Lord Chrysler, David, stood by the fireplace, dressed in jeans and a mocha-colored leather jacket, his blue eyes alert on her.

"Here she is," Susanna said with a vein of excitement.

"Avery, hello." He crossed over to her, his white smile confident. "Sorry to pop by unannounced."

"David, what are you doing here?" Avery glanced at Susanna. *What gives?*

"I came to see if you'd care to go horseback riding. It's always a lovely adventure in the snow. Cold but lovely. Do you ride?"

"No, I don't."

"But she surfs, David. Rather well. If you can stand on a surf board you ought to be able to stay in a saddle, isn't that right, Avery?" Susanna shoved her toward this semi-stranger while quoting a five-year-old conversation they'd had when they flew home from Nathaniel's coronation, fleeing the press.

"Colin was going to take me riding."

"You don't ride." Susanna walked down the airport thoroughfare in her twenty-eight-hundred-dollar Christian Louboutins.

"If I can stand on a board and ride an unpredictable wave, I think I can manage a horse."

"Aves," Susanna said. "We're going home. Stop complaining."

With a sigh, Avery flopped back down to her seat. *"We were living a fairy tale, weren't we? Just for a moment."*

"I concur," David said. "If she can surf she can ride. What do you say, Avery? I'm an excellent instructor. I'll choose the gentlest horse in our mews. We've a path through Aberdeen Forest that takes us to the cliffs. The view is breathtaking."

"Well, I was working—"

"It's Christmas, Aves—" Susanna said.

"—and I'd planned to go shopping." Avery shot David a shy glance. She liked him well enough. But he wasn't Colin.

But for some reason, big sister was all about this date. "We used to gorge on romantic Christmas movies where the hero and heroine took snowy horseback rides."

Susanna! What was she doing? Her pregnancy hormones must be eating her brain.

David laughed low. "I don't know about heroes and heroines, Your Majesty, but the ride is worthy of a film. It's quite beautiful." He peered at Avery without wavering. "I do hope you'll say yes."

"Can I have a moment with my sister?" Avery moved to the door, stepping into the foyer, confronting Susanna when she stepped out after her.

"Why are you pushing me at David?"

"Why are you sitting up in your suite letting your Christmas vacation pass you by? The cliffs are extraordinary. You can worry about a job when you get home. And I don't know what is going on with you and Colin—"

"Nothing."

"Then what's the problem?" She arched her brow, challenging Avery. "Go with David. As a friend, if nothing else, though he is rather good-looking. And you've always wanted to learn to ride."

"I never wanted to learn to ride." Tears always visited at the most unlikely moment. "I merely wanted to ride with Colin. Oh, Suz, Brighton and Colin go together for me. When I'm here, I can't help but think of him. Miss him, if I'm honest. I want to see the cliffs through his eyes. I—"

"Then call him. Ask him to take you."

She shook her head. "I can't risk it."

Susanna wagged her finger. "I knew it. You love him, don't you?"

"Oh my gosh, yes. I do. Are you happy now?" Avery brushed the tears from her cheek. "But I won't come between him and his father. Knowing how I miss Daddy, I can't help but believe Colin would come to resent me."

"Edward can be a hard man, but I can't believe he'd give up a relationship with his son because he married the woman he loves."

"Are we talking marriage, Suz?"

"Avery, sweetie, then go with David. You certainly don't have to marry him. You've the weight of your world on you. Time for some fun. Make new memories. All your concerns will be waiting for you after Christmas."

"Really?" Avery curled her lip. "Can't Santa make them go away?"

Susanna laughed, turning Avery toward the library. "Go. Learn to ride. The cliffs will put you in the Christmas spirit."

David stood when they entered. "Is everything okay?"

"Sorry about that," Avery said. "But yes, I'd love to go horseback riding. Thank you for inviting me. I'll get ready."

"Aves, go in my closet. Get my riding boots and jacket," Susanna said.

"All right!" As Avery reached for the door, Malcolm stepped inside. "Prince Colin calling for Miss Avery."

Colin came through, his cheeks ruddy from the cold, his blue eyes radiating.

"Good afternoon. David! Didn't expect to see you here."

"I've invited Avery to go riding. To see the cliffs."

"Odd that, because I've come to ask her the same."

"You're too late. She's agreed to go with me."

"Colin, Avery was saying she needed to go shopping." Susanna just couldn't stop meddling. "My schedule is so full this week. Could you take her?"

"I'd be delighted."

Delighted? Avery tried not to laugh. The word sounded so foreign on his lips.

"Well, I really need to run." Susanna made a beeline for the door. "Aves, have fun. Good to see you, David . . . and Colin."

And she was alone in the library with her suitors.

"Enjoy your time with David." Colin crossed over to her. "He's a good horseman. I'll see you tomorrow, say ten? We'll go round to the shops. The bakeries are amazing in the morning, full of fresh scents and free samples."

"Ten?" She nodded, watching him, already filled with anticipation. "Perfect."

He shook David's hand and left with a sideways glance at Avery.

"I hope it's okay I'm here," David said when Colin had gone. "I know he was keen on you at one time."

"Years ago."

"What about you? Were you keen on him?"

"I was . . . but now . . . well, I should get ready."

"I meant what I said, Avery." David stepped toward her. "I rather like tall women with auburn hair and a Southern accent."

"David, I'll be going home after New Year's. I'll be four thousand miles away."

He nodded, thinking. "Answer me this. If Colin rang the bell for you, would you marry him on Christmas Day?"

Avery hesitated at the door.

"No matter your answer." David stepped toward the door. "We'll still have a lovely time riding today. No one can be glum in the presence of the cliffs."

Avery hurried to Susanna's apartment. Would she marry Colin if he *really* rang the bell for her? Bet your bottom dollar she'd marry him. In a Georgia minute.

CHAPTER 18

December 20
Five days until Christmas

Jealousy was a cruel companion. Colin had fought the beast all yesterday, trying not to picture Avery with Lord Chrysler, what with his blond hair and charming smile.

Did she fancy him? Colin couldn't see it. David was too perfect. If he could say such a thing about another man. About a rival.

He'd caught a sharp eye from Dad during a conference call when his distracted thoughts drew away his attention.

When he informed his assistant he'd be out all day Tuesday, Dad knocked on his door.

"Where are you going?"

"Christmas shopping?"

"Go when your workday is over. Or on the weekend. Or order online."

"Dad, I'm going shopping." It was a test, really. To stand up to his father. To be his own man.

Before talking to Nathaniel, before realizing the challenge God had *rung* over his life, Colin would've surrendered. Done as his father suggested.

Today, however, he followed his heart and waited for Avery in the parlor of her suite. When she came out of her bedroom, hair flowing over her shoulders, a touch of lip gloss making her lips glisten, love took a deeper root in his heart.

It was more than her beauty. It was her aura.

"Ready?" Colin said.

She took her coat from the closet by the door. "I've been meaning to tell you . . . thanks for the other night, at the symphony. You didn't have to do that."

"My friend was in trouble. What was I to do? Leave her to cry alone?"

"I overreacted."

"Not really. Your heart was hurting." Their eyes met and the matter was settled between them.

"How was your time with David?"

"Fun. Took me a bit to get the hang of riding but my horse got me. David's a very good horseman. The ride through the forest to the cliffs was spectacular. The view was everything David advertised."

"Will you be going with him again?" Colin held open the door for Avery to exit. "My car is in the garage."

"I don't know." She slipped on her coat. "What about you? How are things going with Lady Jordan?"

"We're friends, Avery."

"Does she know that?"

"More than. She's all about her career. She spent the entire evening at the symphony talking to Bobo. To be honest, I think she uses me to run in royal circles."

"Then shame on you for letting her."

She was right. He'd fallen into a routine with Jordan because Dad and Mum liked her.

"I thought we'd go to Old Towne." He glanced at Avery, relaxing, trusting God was directing him in this move. It was a step he needed to take if he was going to win her heart.

She smiled. "Perfect."

In the car and heading out, sans security, Colin moved toward the old city center, the midmorning light still deciding if it would break toward sunshine or clouds.

When he parked, they found their way down the street, leaving the modern world behind for the ancient. As they rounded the corner to start the Old Towne walk, a tender snow began to fall.

Avery stopped at the first decorated window. "This is beautiful."

The display was of an evening snowscape, children skating under the old Braxstone Bridge, their father looking on, smiling. A creative array of white lights portrayed the stars and moon.

"Makes you want to step into it, doesn't it?" Avery said. "To a world where there are no worries or cares, just a kid at Christmas with your dad watching over you."

Colin tapped the window. "Dad used to take my sisters and me skating under that bridge. The water would only freeze in the coldest of winters. Mum would watch from the banks with a tin of hot chocolate, pretending not to fret."

She peered at him. "What a lovely memory."

"What about you? Any fond Christmas memories? Maybe of your dad? I know you miss him."

"I miss him, of course. Nothing feels right without him. I have all sorts of jumbled-up Christmas memories. Closing up the Shack in time for Christmas Eve service. Daddy taking buckets of barbecue sauce and ribs for everyone after." She laughed softly. "The kids would run around the church grounds playing capture the flag or tag, our fingers and faces covered in barbecue sauce. No one yelled at us because it was Christmas." Behind them, shoppers scuttled. "When I was about ten, we were waiting for my aunt and uncle to arrive. It was super cold and they'd gotten caught in snow traffic in North Carolina. Mama was making cookies. Susanna was home from her job in Atlanta. She was twenty-two, out on her own. Whenever she came home, the whole house changed. She just electrified everything."

"She does that now."

"She does, doesn't she? Anyway, the tree was twinkling and, sigh, it was a kid's Christmas. Presents were piled up. We'd been to church and I remember feeling so full of love. So grateful for Jesus. Dad had Bing on the stereo. I'd learned a hand game at school. You know, where you clap hands with another person and sing a silly song. I'd decided to teach Daddy how to play. He kept popping frozen Snicker bites into his mouth, laughing, never getting the rhythm right." Tears glistened in her eyes. "That was a good Christmas."

"Maybe this Christmas will be even better." Colin tucked in next to her, loving this moment between them, loving the sound of her voice in reminiscence. This was how it was between them in the beginning. No barriers. No fears.

"I hope so. I've not done a very good job of enjoying the season so far."

"Come on." He looped his arm through hers. "There's more to see."

As they walked, passersby paused, staring, then found their phones for a photo. But mostly the citizens of Brighton left the prince alone.

The beamed-and-stone buildings faced one another on a narrow, cobbled street. Garland swung from the windows and over the doorways.

Shopkeepers in aprons sold their wares on carts under large, square windowpanes. The produce man called "G'morning" to the keeper of the haberdashery across the way.

"It's like being in another time," Avery said, matching her gait with Colin's.

"The shop owners do a smashing job of keeping it true to history. But this shop"—Colin reached for the door marked Franklin Bakery—"Is my favorite place in Old Towne. Their founder goes way back in Brighton history. We believe with ties to the royal family."

"Don't have to convince me. I love Franklin's."

The shop was warm, filled with the fragrance of baking bread and cinnamon. The stout man behind the counter came around, wiping his hands on his apron. He and his brothers, all Mr. Franklins, ran the five bakeries around the city. The royal family knew every one of them.

"Prince Colin, to what do I owe this pleasure?"

"Mr. Franklin, good morning. We came for some of your good puffs." Colin glanced at Avery. "This is Avery Truitt, Princess Susanna's sister."

"Well sure. I recognize her from her picture. And she's just as lovely as her sister." The man bobbed and bowed. "Now, what can I get you? Puffs? A cuppa? Everything is on the house, of course."

"No, sir, we are patrons and want to pay. Puffs and tea sound good. Avery?"

"Don't have to ask me twice."

"Coming right up and your money's no good here. Won't hear no protests. My Christmas gift to you and yours. Please, sit." Mr. Franklin waved a finger at his four other customers. "No pestering the prince. Or out you go."

Colin nipped curiosity in the bud by greeting the patrons, saying hello, introducing Avery as the princess's sister. "Showing her a bit of our fair city."

That should quell the gossip.

Colin selected a table and held Avery's chair. "Having fun?" he said, sitting across from her.

"More than I want to, yes."

"Don't be stubborn, now. Worry about your job after the New Year."

She sat back, slipping from her coat. "I'd actually forgotten about my job."

"Your Majesty, would you care for hot sourdough as well?" Mr. Franklin appeared over Colin's shoulder. "With fresh jam?"

"Avery?" Colin said. She nodded. "Indeed we would, Mr. Franklin. But please, call me Colin. I'm not Your Majesty."

"Very well. I'll be right back." Mr. Franklin scurried off, waving his finger in the air.

"Why do you correct him?" Avery said. "What does it matter?"

"Because I'm not an HRH, Avery. I am just a mere prince. Uncle Leo didn't think it necessary since I was fifth in line to the throne. He didn't want me to even be a prince. But Dad fought him."

"Really? You never told me."

"Dad's always fought for his family. For what's his."

Mr. Franklin set two plain teacups in front of them, along with a pot of tea. "I'll be right round with your puffs and bread."

"That doesn't mean you have to correct everyone who misspeaks."

"It does to me. It's an honor to be His Royal Highness." Colin reached to pour the tea. "It's a real title. What if David went around calling himself a prince even though he's only an earl?"

"This is why I'm glad to be an American. We're all just 'Hey you over there.'"

He laughed. "You can't mean it. You'd call your president, 'Hey you'?"

She smiled. "Probably not."

"Here we are." Mr. Franklin set a basket of puffs and a basket of bread on the table, shuffling out plates—white with a red-and-green trim, a faded "Merry Christmas from Franklin's Bakery" in the center—and a bowl of jams and butter.

"He really hustles for you," Avery said when he'd gone.

"Well, there are some advantages to being a prince."

Colin filled their cups, asking Avery if she wanted cream. She passed the sugar and fixed their plates with bread and puffs, the rhythm between them easy, familiar. Like they'd shared tea and puffs a thousand times.

Avery popped a puff into her mouth. She hummed, eyes closed, savoring her first bite. "Oh, carbs, why do you taste so good?"

Colin laughed, a sound she adored, and dusted cinnamon from his fingers. Avery reached across, tapping his full cheek with her finger.

"So that's why they're called puffs. They're so good you stuff your mouth until your cheeks puff out."

He nodded, swallowing, taking a sip of tea. "By King Stephen, you've solved a two-hundred-year-old Brighton mystery."

"Oh shush. Don't mock me."

"Mock you?" He pressed his hand to his chest. "Never." Then he peered into her eyes for a long moment. "Is this as fun as riding horses?"

"Colin—"

"Sorry, I withdraw the question."

She sipped her tea, speaking into the steaming brew. "Much better."

When she peeked at him, he winked, and sure as shooting, the bottom dropped right out of her heart.

"So what's on your list for St. Nick this Christmas?" he said.

"I don't know . . ." She sighed. "Something wonderful and romantic? I am in Brighton, after all."

"Well, well." A boisterous voice resonated from the front door. "Fancy meeting you two here." Avery turned to see Guy Smoot and Lady Sarah enter the bakery. "Colin, what are you doing out in the middle of a workweek? Surely your father didn't let you off the ball and chain."

"He didn't have a say in it." Colin stood, shaking his friend's hand and kissing Lady Sarah's cheek. "You both know Avery."

"Of course we do." Guy shook her hand, then leaned over the table with a large sniff. "I'm in heaven. I'll have whatever they're having, Mr. Franklin."

"Shh, Guy, lower your voice." Sarah rolled her eyes at Avery, taking the chair next to her. "Do you mind?"

"Not at all."

Mr. Franklin popped out from the back and hurried to the counter. "What can I do for you?"

"Come help me order, mate." Guy tugged on Colin's arm. "The man worships you." He shuffled to the counter, dragging Colin along with him.

"My apologizes for Guy. He can't contain himself," Lady Sarah said, peeling off her gloves. "He has to do everything with gusto."

"I like that about him." Avery passed Sarah the bread basket. "You have to try this."

She breathed in the aroma. "But oh, the carbs."

"Tell me about it."

Sarah weakened, taking a slice of bread. "It's Christmas, right?"

"Exactly." Avery liked her. She was like a Georgia girl underneath her noble title and Brighton citizenship.

"So what are you and Colin about today?" Sarah spread a thick layer of jam on her bread, then savored her first bite.

"Just shopping."

"I probably shouldn't say this, but when we were in our final year at uni, all Colin ever talked about was you. Even after we graduated, he went on and on about Avery Truitt."

"He couldn't have said much. We weren't a couple all that long."

"Well, to hear him, you two were madly in love."

Avery regarded Lady Sarah for sincerity. "Really?"

She sat back, reaching for a napkin from the dispenser. "I suppose I exaggerate. He didn't talk about you *all* the time, but when he spoke of the girl for him, yes, it was always you."

Avery glanced across the bakery to where Colin stood with Guy, talking, viewing something on their phones.

"Didn't you play some sort of sport for your university?" Sarah said.

"I did. Volleyball."

"Yes, that's right. How could I forget? Colin was obsessed with the sport after he met you. Several of us decided to go on holiday together. To the Mediterranean. He organized a volleyball tournament. It was quite fun."

"Oh, wow, how fun." Lady Sarah was full of secrets Avery loved to hear.

"He never told you? Anyway, I admire you. I don't know how you do all that jumping and spiking." Sarah reached for another slice of bread. "Didn't he ever talk to you about it? How many times did he fly over to watch your matches? Half a dozen?" She looked at Avery, expecting an answer.

"I-I don't know. I didn't keep track." Was she understanding Sarah right? Colin flew to the States to see her play? "Wait, Sarah, who exactly flew over to watch my matches?"

"Colin. Am I right on that? He'd disappear on us every December to watch some NC-something or other tournament."

"NCAA tournament?"

Sarah raised her hand to her mouth as she chewed a bit of jammed bread. "Yes, that's it. You Americans and your acronyms. You're as bad as the Brits. Anyway, he'd go off every year to your matches."

"Sarah, love." Guy turned from the counter. "Do you want coffee or tea?"

"Tea, thank you. And, darling, bring round a basket of sourdough. It's fabulous and I'm going to eat all of Colin and Avery's."

"Your request is my command."

Meanwhile, Colin passed by the table, his phone pressed to his ear. "Be right back. Hello, this is Tattersall." He paced outside, along the sidewalk, pausing to peer through the glass, smiling at Avery when she caught his eye. He attended her games? Without telling her? He hung up after a moment, shivering as he returned to the table. "I believe it's getting colder."

"You went to the NCAA tournament every year?" Avery said.

Colin froze, half standing, half seated, his gaze flipping to Sarah. "What?"

"You flew over to watch my games and never said a word to me?"

"Sarah, what did you say to her?" He stood tall, commanding the room in doing so.

"Oh, blimey, have I let a cat out of a bag?" Innocence filled her shocked expression. "I'm so sorry, darling, but he never spoke a word about its being a secret. We all knew he was madly in love with you." She leaned toward him. "Though now you can't get him to admit it."

"Sarah."

"Well, we did. I'm just going to say it. And the gig with Lady Jordan is up. You know she was out with Clive Boston last night?" Sarah clicked her tongue and tapped Avery on the arm. "He's old enough to be her father."

"Colin, you came to my games?" Avery rose up to meet him. "Why? I-I can't believe you did that."

"Don't be angry."

"I'm not." At least she didn't think so. But she could've seen him. Talked to him. Waved to him from the court.

"I wanted to see you play. I wanted to see with my own eyes what a stellar athlete you are, and how you led your conference in kills."

She regarded him for a moment, then stepped around the table, reaching for his hands. "I can't believe it."

"Yeah, well—"

She pressed her hand to his cheek, her gaze swimming through his. She didn't care any more about the past. About her broken heart. About protocol and the fact they were in a public place with all eyes watching.

"Avery?" Colin furrowed his brow. "Are you all right?"

She slipped her arms around him as if to never let him go, unlocking her heart as she pressed her lips to his. He tasted more delectable than the puffs.

Colin swept his arms about her, taking the kiss to a deeper passion where the bottom dropped out of her world and only Colin remained.

When the kiss finally broke, she tapped her forehead to his. "I'm sorry, Colin, but I have to say it. I love you. Always have. I'm afraid I always will."

"Then we're in the same predicament. Because I love you, Avery. Always have. Afraid I always will."

CHAPTER 19

December 21
Four days until Christmas

Madeline & Hyacinth Live! Show

Hyacinth: "Four days, Hyacinth. Four days. This
is killing me. No hint of a royal Christmas
wedding. No gifted goats bleating from the
palace mews. I'm sad, I tell you. Did you see
Lady Jordan photographed with Clive Boston?
Sheesh, he's old enough to be her father."

Madeline: "Hang on, my dear Hy. I have surprising
news for you. (An image of Colin and Avery
popped up on the screen.) One of our loyal
viewers sent us this yesterday. Seems the

prince has been keeping company with the princess's sister, Avery Truitt. Here they are walking arm in arm in Old Towne."

Hyacinth: (Gasping) "What? You're joking!"

Madeline: "Viewers, our producers are willing to put their money where their hearts are . . . in their wallets. (Laughter rose from the audience.) For any viewer who calls or Facebooks us with a valid tip on Prince Colin and Avery Truitt, you could be eligible to win up to ten thousand pounds." (The audience gasped and applauded)

Hyacinth: "Oh, please call or message us. I'm obsessed with this tradition."

Madeline: "Stay tuned. We'll be right back."

Colin snapped off the television with a glance at his office door. The news was out and he expected Dad to barge in demanding an explanation.

He was grateful for a platonic image of the two of them walking through Old Towne instead of a photo from the Franklin's Bakery kiss.

Colin pinched his lips together. At times, he swore they still buzzed from her touch.

This morning he'd sent a dozen white roses to Lady Sarah as a thank-you for spilling the beans about his secret trips to the States. She did more for him in a five-minute conversation than he'd done by surprising Avery on St. Simons.

After Franklin's, they couldn't be parted. They spent the

day ducking into the shadows to steal kisses, all the while riding the reins on their passion. But Colin wanted her. In every way.

Nathaniel invited him to have dinner with the family and Avery's mama gave him what Avery dubbed the Glo Truitt stink eye.

"What are you doing with my daughter?"

He promised and pledged he was on the up-and-up. He would not hurt her again.

After dinner, they retired to the media room for a Christmas movie, *The Holiday*. Avery sat next to him, curling her body into his, and if the world had ended that moment he'd have died a happy, happy man.

But reality settled in as he walked out to his car, Avery's hand in his. "Colin," she said. "What about your dad?"

"I'll have to talk with him, Avery. But as far as I'm concerned, you are the only one for me. He's going to have to accept the truth."

She nodded, wrapping her fingers around his. "I do not want to come between you. I'll be praying he understands. But I can't . . ." When she lifted her gaze to his, her eyes glistened with love. "I can't deny how I feel."

Colin drew her to him for a kiss. "Nor can I, love. But I need to give him a chance to get on board. I don't want to blindside him."

"What if he absolutely protests?"

"It doesn't change my mind. I have to do what I feel God is calling me to do."

She brushed a tear from under one eye. "I'm scared."

"No, darling, don't be scared."

"Can I really be this happy?"

"Yes, *we* are this happy."

"Colin." She grabbed his hands in hers. "Do you truly believe God rang the bell?"

"I do. He answered my prayer about you, love." He brushed away her trail of tears. "We're going to be together. I promise."

Her kiss was firm, pure, resonating with love. "Then I'll trust you. And God."

With those words, he slept peaceful and deep all night. He woke up smiling.

Colin checked his tie in the mirror over the bookcase and smoothed his hair. The workday was over. Time to speak to Dad.

God, be with me.

Down the hall for the large corner office overlooking the river, Colin peered through Dad's open door. "Got a sec?"

"For you, of course. I was just looking over the union contracts from Hessenberg. It looks like I need another meeting in Hessenberg. I'd like you to go with me. I'm arranging it for Friday, the twenty-third. I know it's holiday time, but if this union contract fails—"

"Dad, can we leave off work for a moment?" Colin took a seat adjacent to the desk. "I need to talk to you about the bell."

Dad set down the contract. "I'm listening."

"That night, when Guy and I were in the tower . . ." He paced, detailing the story to his father. Why did talking to Dad about intimate things like love and God feel uncomfortable? "All that to say, I love her. I want to marry her."

Dad's countenance remained unchanged. So Colin went on.

"I know this is not what you want for me, it's not what we planned, but it's what I want, I believe what God wants."

Dad paced around his desk to the bar against the wall. He reached for a glass and poured a small shot. "Avery knows this?"

"I've not officially proposed, but yes, she knows I love her."

Dad tossed back the drink. "So what do you want from me?"

"I'd like your blessing, but I understand—"

"You just said it, son. This is not what we planned." Dad hammered his glass against the bar top. "Colin, consider your future. You are a royal. A man of industry." He swung his arm wide, toward the office. "All this will be yours one day."

"How does that preclude me from marrying Avery?"

"Doesn't she want to be a coach? How will she do that here?"

"Volleyball is a growing sport, Dad. We'll find a way. But that doesn't change how we feel. What we know is right."

"Poppycock. All well and good until she wakes up one day and realizes she's given up everything for you. You saw how her sister ran off on Nathaniel when she had to give up everything."

"That's not fair. She had to give up her citizenship. Avery won't have to do that. Even if she did—"

"Do you want to face divorce one day? Scandal."

"Dad, she wanted to marry me five years ago. She already wanted to give up everything."

"You were children."

"Well, we're not now. We know what we want."

"Love is blind. How can you know—"

"Love is also eye-opening. I can be more of who you want me to be with Avery than Lady Jordan, trust me."

"So you're going against me."

"Dad, I don't want to go against you. I've always followed your wisdom and advice, but this time I must follow my heart. I must follow the Lord. He's speaking to me directly now and not through you. Or Mum."

"Mum will be devastated. She loves Lady Jordan."

"She loved Avery when she first met her too."

Dad started to pour another shot but put the decanter down. "Then will you give it time? See what the new year brings. Then if you feel the same this time next year, I'll support you."

"I can't do that. I said to the Lord that if I could marry Avery, I'd launch the Pembroke traditions. And He responded by ringing the bell Himself. I'm going to marry her at Watchman Abbey Christmas morning."

Dad locked his hands behind his back, facing the windows to the city. "When will you announce?"

"First I need to properly ring the bell. I know ringing it this late is not the tradition, but I need to keep my word to the Lord. I need to do it for Avery. I have some things to organize, but I plan to ring it day after tomorrow. Then propose."

"The twenty-third? I want to leave for Hessenberg on the eight o'clock ferry."

"Absolutely. I'm your man, Dad. I'll ring the bell at first light, then meet you. I just need to return on the two o'clock ferry. I have plans to propose that evening."

He had it all organized. At least in his head. He'd invite Avery to meet him in the quiet, romantic Old Towne Square Friday at sundown. There, he'd propose.

Dad's jaw knotted as he nodded. "If you've made up your mind."

"I have. Can we keep this between us? I don't want the press or anyone finding out before Avery."

His father hesitated, then nodded. "Very well."

Colin pumped his fist on his way back to his office. It wasn't all he wanted from Dad, but more than he expected.

Now to get truly organized. First stop? Lord & Gladwell to retrieve Granny's engagement ring.

Then he had to see a man about some goats.

Edward swirled another shot of golden brew in his glass and stared out his window, considering his options. God rang the bell? Indeed. If he didn't know better he'd think his son had gone mad.

Colin was a steady chap. True blue, that one. Yet in the matter of Avery Truitt, he was soft. What he needed was a solid wake-up call. Edward suspected the Truitt girl did as well.

She belonged in America. And Colin belonged in Brighton with a Brightonian woman.

Returning to his desk, Edward reached for the phone, hesitated, then dialed. He didn't want to do this but desperate measures must be taken. "Madeline Stone please. Edward Tattersall calling."

CHAPTER 20

December 22
Three days until Christmas

"Excuse me, Miss Avery?" Malcolm stood in the entryway to the dining room. "There's a delivery for you."

"For me?" Avery peeked at Susanna and Mama as she wiped her lips with a very fine linen napkin and scooted away from the table. "What kind of delivery?"

"Very unusual. I've never seen anything like it."

"Malcolm, what is it?" Nathaniel said.

"You'll have to see for yourself, sir."

"Curiouser and curiouser, Malcolm." Avery glanced back at the family as she followed the butler. "I'll be back."

Down the back stairs to the kitchen and out the back door, Avery halted at the bleating rising in the shadows of the palace lights.

"Malcolm?" She squinted into the darkness.

"These arrived for you." He motioned to the man waiting. "Come on out."

Colin, dressed in a tweed suit and leather knee boots, stepped forward, pulling along two rather adorable, protesting goats, a leash in each hand. "Hello, Avery. I'd like you to meet Fred and Ethel."

"Oh my word." She dropped to one knee, extending her hand, touching their noses. "Goats? Colin, what is this?"

"A typical gift from the suitor who rang the bell."

Avery rose up, her warm skin oblivious to the cold. "What are you saying?"

"Should we call for Glo? Have her accept my offer of two goats for one daughter."

"Colin, don't joke with me."

"Am I laughing? Malcolm, my man, shall we deliver these to the stable?" He held up the leashes.

But Malcolm recoiled. "I've already called for the groomer."

"Fair enough." With the bleating of scared, hungry goats in the air, Colin pulled Avery to him. "Meet me in the Old Towne Square tomorrow at sundown, by the decorated tree. I'll send a car for you."

"Colin, you're making me fall more in love with you." She shivered against him.

"'Tis my plan."

"Are you really sure? Did you talk to your father? What did he say?"

He kissed her forehead, then her cheek, working toward her lips. "You ask too many questions."

"Because I'm serious." She pushed from his arms. "I really want your father to be on our side."

"That's his choice." He clasped her hand in his. "But this time is about you and me, about what we want. I was thinking about the school you aided in their volleyball game. Perhaps you can offer your expertise to them. Join them as a coach. If they snub you, we'll move on to another school. We'll start a volleyball camp. Love, whatever you want—"

"Colin, you haven't even asked me anything yet. Not officially."

He wrapped her up, laughing. "Right you are. So, the Old Towne Square tomorrow? Sundown."

"All right." She pressed her hands against his chest. "I'll be there tomorrow." Her countenance darkened. "If you're sure. Colin, are you sure?"

He smoothed his hand along the lean line of her jaw. "Avery, I realize I've let you down. I broke your heart. But not this time. You can trust me. I give you my word I'll be there tomorrow night." The goats bleated, demanding attention. "See, even the goats agree."

"And every night after?" Avery laughed as Fred, or was it Ethel, pushed against her leg.

Colin grinned, cupping her face in his hand and warming her heart with his kiss. "Yes, and every night after."

"Then I'll be there." Because all she really wanted for Christmas was Prince Colin Tattersall of Brighton.

December 23
Two days until Christmas

At first light, Colin moved carefully up the chapel steps, his torch waving over the smooth steps, the strap of his rucksack secure on his shoulder.

In it he had the most important thing he needed for the

evening, Granny's ring—a ten-karat piece of sapphire and diamond set in filigree platinum. It was lovely. Stunning, if a chap could say so.

She'd been Lady Eugenia, a gorgeous redhead with fire in her eyes when Great-Granddad, Prince Fritz, proposed. They were known for their love and devotion to one another.

Colin hoped to follow in their footsteps.

He'd only been a tot of one year when Granny died, bequeathing him her engagement ring. Now, as a man on the verge of his own romantic journey, his affection rose for the wise woman who looked down the generations and offered a piece of herself.

Nearing the top of the tower, anticipation thudded in his chest. He was about to ring the bell for his true love. Avery was going to be his.

What kindness God showed him. Bringing him Avery for his Christmas. A man had no quarrel with a Redeemer who satisfied his soul with a good thing.

With a deep inhale, Colin arrived at the top, a sharp, strong wind billowing through the archways. Of course, there remained a small sliver of doubt Avery would refuse him.

She had a night to think about her future, talk with Susanna about being a princess in a foreign land.

Colin half made up his mind if Avery wanted to live in America and coach, then he'd resign his post at Tattersall Ltd. and move to the States.

Surely he could find a position somewhere. Or take part of Tattersall Ltd. with him. Dad had more than enough connections.

Unhooking the bell cord from the wall, Colin created three loops on the end, holding them in one hand while gripping the middle in the other.

If he remembered his youth training, ringing up a bell began with a firm tug, then letting the rope slip through his hands, higher and higher until he worked through the coils.

"For You, Lord." Colin put his full body, his whole heart, into ringing the heavy bell. "And for Avery."

The rope bounced as the bell began to ring, chiming out love, calling out a destiny. The rope slid through his hands, and he let out the first coil, then the next, the bell's clanging reverberating through him, taking on a life of its own, swinging and ringing.

Colin skipped to the open arch and faced the city, arms wide.

"I'm in love!" The knelling rolled over the low hills covered in white. "Ha-ha!"

He had no time to linger. He must meet Dad at the ferry. Grabbing his torch, hitching the strap of the rucksack higher on his shoulder, he started down.

The narrow stairwell echoed with the call of the bell. As Colin drove down to the dock, the tolling followed him.

As he parked, the sun peeked through scattering snow clouds and glinted against his windshield. Colin grabbed his rucksack and headed to the ferry, skipping through the swaths of light, feeling free and confident.

By King Stephen I, he'd make the three o'clock ferry. He must! Colin ran for the dock, his rucksack anchored on his shoulder, Dad dallying behind him.

He'd missed the one o'clock departure. And the two. If he missed this one, Avery would be standing in Old Towne Square alone, wondering what happened to him, the sun already setting.

The plan was no communication until he walked up to her, ring in hand, dropping to one knee, asking, "Will you marry me?"

But everything about this day dragged. No one was on time. Conversations meandered. The negotiations took three hours instead of the anticipated one. Yet the rest of the diplomacy was tedious and demanding. Lunch was carried in yet the hours ticked-tocked away.

"Excuse me, excuse me." Colin squeezed past the stragglers and other last-minute passengers only to find himself in a queue to go down the ramp. Tugging his phone from his pocket, he started to dial Avery. He had to break silence to let her know he'd be a little late . . .

A hand pressed him from behind. "The line is moving."

Colin stumbled forward, his hand cracking against the cold metal railing at such an angle his phone shot free, arching keenly toward the water.

"No! No!" Colin reached, scraping the air in hopes of nabbing his phone. But the device was far beyond his fingertips.

How could such an expensive phone make such a pitiful, insignificant splash?

"My phone." Blue words blistered his tongue. *Don't say them. Sure as you do, someone will note you are Prince Colin.*

Dad eased alongside him, clapping his hand against his arm. "I told you we had plenty of time."

Frustration steamed under Colin's skin as he filed onto the ship and took a seat across from Dad, anxiety knotting every part of him. Thank God he'd only lost his phone. And not the rucksack. He'd dive into the freezing water to save Granny's ring.

"Might I borrow your iPad?" Of all times for Dad not to have a cell phone.

Giving him the eye, Dad passed it over, then reached for the folded *Informant* someone left on the seat beside him. "What's going on?"

"You know what's going on. I'm supposed to meet Avery." Colin reminded Dad of his plan—the hundred and forty character version—while searching through his contacts, formulating yet another plan.

E-mail Nathaniel or Susanna, have them get in touch with Avery. But the royal e-mail addresses were not in Dad's system.

Colin peeked at his father. "Where are the family e-mail addresses?"

"Different iPad." Dad reached for the device. "I don't mix business with pleasure. This is a Tattersall machine. I don't put personal contacts in with my business ones."

Colin sighed, tipping back his head. "This is a nightmare." He glanced around. Maybe he could borrow another passenger's phone. Except he didn't have any of the numbers he needed memorized.

"She'll understand if you're late."

"No, she won't." Colin clinched his reply through a taut jaw. "Frankly, she shouldn't be required to understand. I stood her up once, and now she's going to think I'm doing it again."

"Then she's not the woman you think she is."

"She's everything I think she is. Trouble is, I'm being the man she *thinks* I am. The one she fears I am." He hammered the table, then glared at his father. "You wanted this to happen, didn't you?"

"That's unfair. Of course not. I don't want the girl hurt."

"But you don't mind if she's upset with me. Angry. Probably won't want anything to do with me."

"What's confusing to you, Colin? I've not changed my mind

about who you should marry. I do not believe an American is best for you, our family, or our country."

"Dad, my wife is for me. Not you, the family, or even the country. If you were honest with yourself, I'm not really a royal with any pull—"

Dad slammed the table this time. "I'll not hear you talk this way. You have much royal pull and power."

"Dad—" Colin leaned in to catch his eye and draw a sincere response. "Did you sabotage my proposal? Drag out the day to make me late?"

"Don't put this on me, lad. If you needed to depart, then why didn't you get up and leave?"

He sat back. "Because . . ." His sigh released only an ounce of his burden. "We were with business partners—the union leaders. I respect them, and you, too much to just walk away. I don't want to cast dispersions on the company or our reputation. By the way, you did an amazing thing today, winning over the labor union president."

Dad turned the pages of the paper. "Colin, perhaps you didn't leave because you realize, deep down, that I'm right, again, about this lass. She's not the girl for you. I get it, son; she's beautiful and alluring. Something happens to your brain whenever she's around. I had a woman like that in my life before I met your mum. But she was not my future."

"You're wrong. Avery is my future." Colin stared out the ferry window as the sun set beyond the horizon, taking his aspirations of the day with it. "What I'd like to know is why you didn't call the lunch? You knew I needed to get on or risk being late."

"I was doing business. And I never rush when doing business." Dad flipped through the pages of the *Informant*.

"Twice now, due to you, I've let her down. The first time you were right. We were too young, with too much schooling ahead of us. This time you're wrong. Perhaps you did not delay lunch on purpose, perhaps you did. But, Dad, hear me now, I will marry Avery. If not this Christmas Day, then the next."

The tension between the men, father and son, threaded through Colin. He'd never spoken to Dad with such frankness. It bothered him. But he was right.

The rest of the way home he prayed for Avery. Prayed for himself. Trusting the One who rang the bell for him when his heart was too weak to know its own way.

She loved sunsets. The fact that a brilliant glow rimmed the horizon as the driver steered the Mercedes sedan down the tight Old Towne streets on her way to meet Colin inspired an array of chills over her skin.

Susanna and Mama were certainly excited. Mama loved the goats. But Avery kept a lid on her expectations. She'd been here before with Colin—close enough anyway—and he shut her out.

This morning she woke with apprehension. How could it be that the secret desire of her heart was coming true? Surely she was just imagining it.

Did Colin really want to marry her? Or was tonight simply a romantic Christmas date?

Then the chapel bell rang this morning and she knew—

He's going to propose.

Mama and Susanna were out all day with a doctor's appointment and last-minute Christmas shopping, and Avery used her morning to dream and nap.

But by mid-afternoon, she was restless so she dressed for a run in the cold and took off down Stratton Boulevard, a protection officer following in a warm car.

She returned with enough time to shower and ready for the sunset date. She went casual, with a pair of jeans, a pale-green sweater, and black boots. She borrowed Susanna's John Lewis cream coat with the dark-brown faux fur.

She curled her hair. Wore makeup. Tried to look like the girl Colin fell in love with five years ago. Only older and wiser.

The car picked her up at three fifteen. Sunset came early on the island. Approaching Old Towne Square, the driver slowed, passing through the warm squares of shop light, then stopped. Getting out, he opened Avery's door and offered his hand as she stepped out, tipping his hat.

"The square is across the avenue, miss." He pointed straight ahead.

Avery inhaled, hand pressed to her middle where butterflies and bees collided. "Do I tip you?" She pulled the wristlet from her coat pocket, though she had brought only her phone and twenty quid.

"No, ma'am. The prince has seen to me."

"Then, thank you."

The driver ducked away and Avery headed forward with the sounds and fragrances of the ancient quarter of Cathedral City as her escort.

Shoppers skirted past. A speeding lorry nearly splashed her with a glob of snow. The shop at the end of the street played "Joy to the World" through a small speaker set on a table.

At the corner, Avery watched the traffic, crossing when the road was clear, following Colin's instructions to wait in the center by the decorated tree.

When she arrived, her lungs heaved as if she'd sprinted a marathon. Oh, she was so nervous. *Steady, Aves.*

During tournaments, she had nerves of steel. But a marriage proposal was nothing like a tourney, was it?

Standing in the glow of the tree, she scanned the square to the perimeter, her heartbeat keeping time with the heel clicks of passersby. One of them would be Colin. Would he come from ahead, or surprise her from behind?

Seconds ticked into minutes. Avery checked her phone for the time. The crowd thinned. The town's hurried pace slowed. The sun inched farther down to the west.

Avery walked to the other side of the tree. A TV truck pulled alongside the square. Another passed by with the smiling faces of Madeline and Hyacinth on its side.

A cluster of the curious gathered around her.

Colin, where are you?

She'd not told Susanna where she was going, so no protection officer accompanied her.

Her nerves fired. Was she safe? Where was Colin? Avery clutched her wristlet close, ready to go for her phone.

"You're her, aren't you?" The voice came from the back of the crowd. "The princess's sister."

Avery turned her back, dialing Colin. But his phone went to voice mail.

Onlookers continued to press for information. "Miss Avery, are you waiting for Prince Colin? Did he ring the Pembroke bell this morning?"

Her shivers of excitement turned to shivers of dread. To her left, a commotion split the crowd as Madeline and Hyacinth came through with their camera crew.

Hyacinth, or was it Madeline, spotted her, smiling, and gave Avery two thumbs up. The other TV host hurried over, asking in a loud whisper, "Is he on his way?"

"How did you know?"

"We heard the bell." She laughed, her expression made up for television. "Well, and someone gave us a tip."

"A tip? Who?"

But the glamorous presenter ignored her. "We're so excited about the bell tradition and a Christmas wedding."

"Who said there was going to be a Christmas wedding?"

She squinted, hemming. "Isn't there? We heard he was proposing."

Avery clutched her cold hands into fists. *Oh, Colin, what have you done?*

"We'll be right over here. Oh, I'm Madeline, by the way." The woman offered her slender hand. Avery gave it a light shake, then stepped into the shadows of the giant Christmas tree.

O Christmas tree, O Christmas tree, hide me from my humiliation.

The crowd thickened. The day dimmed and the old street gaslights brightened. Still no Colin.

Madeline and Hyacinth talked between themselves, glancing back at Avery, their expressions morphing from excitement to curiosity to worry to *oh blimey.*

Facing the tree, Avery tried Colin again. No answer.

"Has he stood you up?" Another voice from the crowd.

"Avery." Madeline approached. "Can we get a few words on camera?"

"Happy Christmas." She headed around the tree, away from this present humiliation. But she was encircled by the crowd. And they called to her.

"Can you tell us why you're here?"

"Who rang the bell? Was it for you?"

"Where's Prince Colin?"

She ducked through the crowd, picking up her pace, stepping into the road without looking. This was the last time Prince Colin made a fool out of her.

CHAPTER 21

She spewed. Fumed. Spilling everything to Susanna as she paced her princess sister's living room, the tree in the corner releasing the perfume of pine, the lights too merry for Avery's dark heart.

"He stood me up, Susanna." Avery trembled as she stormed round in a circle. "He tipped off Madeline and Hyacinth but never showed." She paused, hands gripping the side of her head. "Who does that?"

Her anger burned and blazed, spoiling the atmosphere, spoiling her own soul. But oh, she needed to be ticked off for a good long minute.

"Avery, he did not set you up. On purpose? Something must have happened." Susanna blew a low breath over the surface of her steaming tea.

"Yeah, his dad happened. Like last time." She stuffed her hands into her pockets and stared out the window, the lit grounds so dynamic against the dark nights. But she was sick of this rant. She whirled around to Susanna. "How was your doctor's appointment?"

She smiled. "Mama got to hear the heartbeat. Aves, aren't you hungry? Malcolm saved a plate for you." Susanna's wrinkled expression relayed her concern as she called down to the kitchen from her phone, asking for Avery's dinner to be brought up.

As a matter of fact, she was starved. Mad made her hungry. Avery curled up on the sofa next to her sister. "I'm glad about the baby. What do you want, a boy or girl?"

"I know it's cliche but I want healthy." Susanna laughed softly, smoothing her hand over her sister's arm. "Aves, I'm sure there's—"

"A logical explanation? Sure. Why not? Colin's a good guy."

"He can't have done this on purpose. He's not that stupid. Or cruel. Look at you, you're making me defend him and I'm on your side. I'm ticked he didn't show tonight. But I won't go so far as to say he's scheming. There's no reason for it. What's his motivation?"

"His father." There, a perfectly logical explanation. "Colin is his own man except when it comes to his father. He'll do whatever he tells him, justifying it by believing it's all for my good too."

"Edward? He's crafty and calculating, but not cruel."

"Don't you see? He doesn't see it as cruel. When he admonished Colin not to attend my prom, he thought he was doing us all a big favor."

"Colin was in deep. He was losing focus. So were you. I think Edward had a bit of a point. Then. But not now. Surely."

Avery regarded Susanna. "Colin was going to propose, Suz. After prom. He was going to propose."

"What? Really?"

"Edward found out. That's why he didn't come. Why he cut me off cold." Emotion watered Avery's words. "I know it sounds crazy but we would've made it, Susanna. I just know it."

Avery's sob bent her forward, her face in her hands. "I do love him. I can't help it."

"Oh, Aves, sweet Aves." Susanna cradled her, shushing her tears, kissing the top of her hair. "Colin will come along with an explanation. I'm sure of it."

Avery raised her head, swiping away her tears. "Oh, what does it matter? We're not meant to be, Suz. I can't go through this again."

A knock resounded from the door to the servants' hallway. Susanna rose up, beckoning them in.

A young lad with neat blond hair entered with a tray. "For Miss Avery."

"Thank you, Fin."

Susanna motioned for Avery to sit. Eat. "Come on. Food will do you good. Chef made a lovely cream beef stew and hot buns. We can cue up *It's a Wonderful Life* and forget about boys for a while."

The fragrance of the stew was enticing, but Avery wasn't so hungry after all. She stared at the food tray, took a sip of the diet soda from the brimming, frothy glass, then set it aside.

"I think I'll go for a walk. I need to think. Pray."

"All right." Susanna squeezed her arm. "He'll call or something. I know he will."

Avery reached for her coat and scarf. "What does it matter? I'm done." She tugged on her gloves.

"Let's trust the Lord's plan. Maybe Colin has a solid explanation."

"You're more of a dreamer than I am, Suz. Edward wants a Brighton woman for his son, the heir to the Tattersall dynasty, a future member of parliament. And he's won. Another American in the family is too bourgeois for him."

"Well, you have this all settled. You've made up Colin's mind for him. You know what he did and why, and have come to a conclusion for him. Why bother to even pray?"

Avery made a face. "I thought you were on my side."

"I am. But let Colin speak for himself. Give God a chance to work this. I certainly remember an exuberant seventeen-year-old admonishing me with the same wisdom when I gave up hope on Nathaniel."

"Fine, he can speak for himself." Avery slipped on her coat. "But *my* mind is made up. He could show up with a diamond ring, a dozen roses, and the Ohio State marching band playing 'I Can't Live If Living Is Without You' and my answer would still be 'No way, no how.'"

"Glad you're keeping an open mind. Wouldn't want anyone to think you're bullheaded."

"Suz, I just want to have a good Christmas and go home. In fact, I'd go home now if Mama wasn't having such a good time."

Susanna drew her into a hug. "It would break my heart, and Nathaniel's, if you left. He feels horrible about all this."

"And if he were a real king, he'd throw Colin in the dungeon."

"Funny." Susanna walked Avery to the door. "Be safe out there. Don't leave the grounds. If you go down the back stairs, you'll open into the private garden by Nathaniel's office."

"I'll be back. Then we can have that lovely beef stew and watch *It's a Wonderful Life*, okay?"

"Aves, if he'd showed and proposed, were you going to say yes?"

She nodded. "Absolutely."

"Wouldn't that have been lovely?"

"Yes, very, very lovely."

Surely heaven and hell were in a war over his heart. Over his love life. First the delays in Hessenberg. Then the disastrous splash of his phone in the North Sea followed by Dad's lack of personal information on his iPad.

Now he was stuck in a Cathedral City Christmas traffic jam that the devil himself must have organized.

Colin mashed his car horn, lips tight, every muscle in his body taut.

He'd called the office from the port, but every admin still working this Christmas holiday had already left. And the office was closed until after New Year's.

Which meant the King's Office was also closed.

Traffic inched forward. Colin advanced thirty yards toward the palace. She probably wouldn't speak to him, and blast if he wouldn't blame her.

Note to self: memorize phone numbers and e-mail addresses.

Spying a side street devoid of a traffic conundrum, Colin zipped out of traffic, racing down the narrow avenue, a bit of freedom releasing in his heart. *Now we're getting somewhere.*

But no. Of course. The side street streamed into another blocked and jammed thoroughfare. Every citizen in Cathedral City was heading toward some holiday affair—shopping, maybe going north to the mountains, to family and friends, or attending a church program . . . the list was endless.

And he was caught in the heart of it all. Colin dropped his head to the steering wheel. "Avery," he whispered. "I'm so sorry."

A faint sound reverberated through him. The memory of the clanging and calling Pembroke bell, ringing from the inside out.

He lifted his head. Why was he sitting around waiting for life to come to him, depending on modern conveniences and devices?

Glancing in the rearview, he reversed into a tight parking slot on the street, half on the cobblestone, half on the sidewalk. Cutting the engine, he snatched up his rucksack, wrapped on his muffler, and alarmed his car.

He was an athlete. Used to be anyway. The five-mile hike to the palace would do him good and it would be faster than staying in this traffic.

"Sir, you can't park your car here." Colin turned to see a constable making his way down the walk on horseback. "No parking after four." He pointed to the sign.

"Begging your pardon, but I am late for a very important date."

"So is half the city. You still can't park your car here."

"Do you know who I am?" Blimey, he'd never said that in all his born days.

The constable grinned. "I thought it was you but wasn't sure. Prince Colin? Good to meet you. But you still can't leave your car here."

"I must get to the palace. I must." Avery would be home, having left the square by now.

"Is everything all right?"

Colin sighed, gripping the strap of his rucksack, hanging on for dear life. "In the grand scheme of things, yes, everything is all right. In the realities of my life, no, everything is a mess. I've mucked this one up for sure."

"Sounds serious."

"If you think breaking your word to the love of your life is serious, then yes."

"Well, I suppose you could order me off my horse in the name of the king. After all, we are the royal mounted and under his command." The constable slipped from his ride. "And I suppose you could hand me the keys to your motor and I could move it for you when the traffic died away." He paused, regarding Colin. "I suppose that's what you're asking me to do, being as there's some royal emergency at the palace."

Colin gaped at him, then said, "Yes, indeed. Give me your mount, Constable . . ."—he read the name on his uniform—"Smithers. In the name of the king." He grabbed the man by the shoulders, kissed him on the cheek, and launched into the saddle. "You'll be properly rewarded for your service." He tossed him his keys. "I'll have security on the alert for you. Your mount will be in the mews."

"Merry Christmas, Your Majesty."

"I'm not Your . . . oh, never mind. Merry Christmas to you too."

Colin reined his ride toward the main avenue, urging him on, the horse galloping boldly through traffic toward the palace, toward love and a princely save worthy of the fairy tales.

CHAPTER 22

The garden scene was serene and beautiful. Peaceful. Susanna had decorated it for Christmas, trimming all the trees and their bare branches in white lights with red winter flowers covering the ground along the sidewalk.

Pulling on her gloves, Avery hunched against the sharp edge of the air and headed down the concrete path, passing under the magical lights.

What was it about lights that made the world magical? Avery loved that Jesus was light. *The* Light.

She paused at the garden gate and gazed out at the snow-covered grounds, the landscape flowing and dipping into light and shadow. *Oh Lord, I need Your light.*

Ahead the scene was dark with a rim of Christmas stars arching over the tallest trees. Behind her was the lit palace, the enormous stone and concrete that housed everyone she loved most in this world.

If this was all she had for the rest of her life, she would be one of the most blessed women in the world. Mama and Susanna, Nathaniel, everyone back home, all her Christmas memories with Daddy and the family.

She'd done well, plain ole Avery Truitt from St. Simons. If this was all God ever blessed her with, she'd be grateful.

She closed her eyes and was eight again, bouncing around the house, waiting for Susanna to come home for the holiday, the tree lights bouncing off the walls and ceiling, a fire crackling in the corner fireplace, Johnny Mathis singing "Winter Wonderland." Bing crooning "White Christmas."

Avery inhaled the cold fragrance of the snow.

Her memory moved to the kitchen and Daddy filling the house with yummy aromas. Mama sitting at the dining room table with the aunts and uncles, Granny and Gramps, laughing.

She opened her eyes. She wasn't eight or ten or twelve any longer, was she? She was twenty-two and life wasn't sweet and innocent, or fairy tales with princes riding up on white steeds to save the day.

"Lord, I don't know what You're up to, but here's the deal. I'm going to trust You. You love me, You're good, and You have amazing plans for me."

Though her confession felt far, far from her heart, she willed her soul to believe what was true, not what she felt, not what she experienced. She blew out a long icy breath. Faith wasn't easy.

But it was Christmastime and she refused to be in the doldrums. Susanna was right. Somewhere along here Colin would come up with some explanation. She'd accept his apology—nothing more—and go home with a sense of closure.

If he proposed she'd not accept him. The night and the cold helped her decide. This kind of stuff would just keep happening. She was right not to come between Colin and his father.

The gate gave way when Avery leaned against it, so she exited out of the garden into the snap of a cold breeze.

"Avery!"

She turned at the sound of thunder over the crunching snow, a rider coming toward her, the power of a dark horse moving over the white grounds. "Avery!"

"David?"

The horse reared as the rider reined him to a stop and dropped out of the saddle.

"I'm sorry, Avery, I'm sorry."

"Colin—"

He took hold of her, his warm lips grazing her cheek. "I'm so, so sorry."

She leaned back, trying to see his face in the ghostly light bouncing off the snow. "Where have you been?"

"Hessenberg. Meeting. Long luncheon, very long. Late to the ferry. Dropped my phone in the water." He gasped, then went on. "Dad has no personal contacts on his iPad, meanwhile my brain was sinking to the bottom of the North Sea. Then there was traffic. Unbelievable Christmas traffic. I never knew it to be so insane. I was five miles and five hours from the palace."

The horse stamped and shuddered, tossing his head, his breath billowing white clouds as if to say, "It's true."

"So you rode a horse?"

"Constable . . . I commandeered him in the name of the king."

She pressed her fingers to her lips, trying not to laugh. "I see . . ."

Colin bent forward for a good long inhale. "I think I've been holding my breath since we left the luncheon."

"So you were late to the ferry, lost your phone, and got stuck in traffic."

"Avery, I never ever meant to leave you standing in Old Towne Square alone."

"With Madeline and Hyacinth looking on?"

"What?"

"They showed up. Wanted a live remote of whatever was going down between you and me. It was humiliating."

"How did they . . ." He exhaled, pressing his lips taut, shaking his head. "Dad. This bears his mark."

Avery crossed her arms. "So, we're really back to where we left off, aren't we?"

"I can't believe he'd do such a thing." Colin paced off a few steps, then came around to Avery. "But again, when Dad wants his way, he'll pull out all stops." He took ahold of her arms. "He's not going to come between us this time."

"Colin, do you think, really, we're not meant to be? Maybe we should just give it up."

"No, no, love, I refuse. The more we are tested, the more I've come to believe we are meant to be. I rang the bell this morning for you. Just like you said. God may have been the one to set our course in motion, but I'm coming round, falling in line with Him."

"I heard the bell, Colin. Then you never showed."

"But I'm here now. You must believe me. Please." His voice pleaded, his expression begged. How could she refuse him?

"All right, I believe you, Colin. I do. But I'm not sure my heart can take—"

"Be mine, Avery. Won't you? I love you so ardently." He held her hands in his, then bent to kiss her, his lips warming away her cold doubts.

When he broke away, she clung to him. "You are winning me over, Colin."

"Good. Because I've a plan."

"Another one?" She pressed her hand to her heart. "I can't endure another plan."

His laugh rang out, rivaling the joy of the cathedral bells. "Trust me, this one is all on you. I'm going to give you a chance to set me up. Test me for a change."

"What? Why would you do such a thing? There's no revenge in forgiveness."

"I'm not talking revenge. But I've publicly embarrassed you."

"You didn't publicly embarrass me."

"But I have. Everyone knew I was to come to your prom. And I never showed. Then you tell me Maddie and Hy ran a live remote at the square . . . Half of Brighton saw you waiting there, alone." He stood back with a pop of his gloved hands. "I'm going to give you a chance to publicly respond to me. It might be good. It might be bad." He made such a face she couldn't help but laugh. "I'll take my chances."

"How? When?"

"Tomorrow. Christmas Eve."

"Colin, please, haven't we had enough back and forth? Let's just pass the day in peace. Tomorrow will be a long day what with the family Christmas breakfast and church that evening. I have a last-minute fitting for my Christmas Ball gown—which I don't want to do but Susanna's designer insists."

"Don't worry, you'll know exactly what I mean tomorrow." Colin slipped his arm around her, finding her lips for a passionate kiss.

The horse whinnied, shoving Colin in the back, forcing him forward so he tumbled into Avery. They tumbled, laughing, into the snow.

For a long moment she didn't move, just breathed in the pleasure of being in his company. Colin gripped her hand and they lay side by side, watching the stars, the constable's mount standing guard.

Christmas Eve
One day until Christmas

A fitting at four on Christmas Eve was not Avery's idea of getting into the holiday spirit. But it was for the Christmas Ball. Ferny promised to be "quick about it."

"I just want to make sure it's right."

Susanna defended her, saying she was nervous to have her first dress for a royal go public at the Christmas Ball.

In the dressing room Avery changed quickly and moved out to the showroom, stepping up on the pedestal so Ferny could inspect every inch.

She'd not stopped smiling since Colin galloped away from her last night, and seeing him at breakfast made her flush with desire.

However, he didn't linger long at the palace, hurrying off with a short good-bye and a whisper.

"Be near a telly at four."

"A telly? Why?"

But he was off before she could protest. Her dress fitting was at four.

With a deep breath, she viewed herself in the mirror, smoothing her hand over the wool and silk skirt, layered in vertical scallops like drifts of snow. The train spread across the dry, beat-up hardwood floor. The sleeveless bodice was covered with pearls and tulle, creating a crew neck just below her collarbone. Her hair, done for church, draped over her shoulders in long waves.

A tremor started from deep inside. This was a wedding dress. *Her* wedding dress.

What could he possibly have planned for his public humiliation?

"What's wrong?" Ferny looked up, her French accent heavy with worry. "You don't like it?"

"No, no, I love it." Avery smiled. "Takes my breath away." She glanced at the clock. The big hand was nearly on the four. "Do you have a TV, Ferny?"

"What? A telly? Over there." She pointed to an old TV set sitting in a wooden case like Grandpa used to have above his garage workbench. "Avery, this gown is stunning on you. I've never designed a gown quite like this one and I'm every bit as proud as I am nervous. Your sister thinks I should make it into a wedding gown line." Ferny moved around the gown, sticking pens into the bodice, fitting it to Avery's waist.

"Y-you should. She's got a very keen eye. Can we turn on the TV?"

"I love her gardens. So I believe you. Now, let me finish this and I can put it away until after Christmas." She sighed. "My husband accuses me of loving my dresses more than him. Now what is it you want? The telly?"

"Avery, what's going on?" Susanna said.

"Colin told me to be near a TV at four." She pointed to the clock.

As Ferny raised the skirt to work, revealing the blue tulle underneath holding out the skirt's many layers, the bells on the front door clattered.

"Turn on the telly. Turn it on now." Ferny's assistant blasted into the showroom, flustered, waving her hands in the air. "Ferny, where's the remote, where's the remote?" She was tall and lanky, with one side of her hair pink and the other side red. Bangles clattered down her arm from her wrist to her elbows.

"Melba, darling, there's no remote. What's all the bother?" Ferny pointed to the telly in the corner, dusty and dark.

Melba hovered over the box, searching, looking. "How do you turn the blooming thing on? It's going to be too late, oh my stars, it's going to be too late."

"You're scaring me. What's going on? Please, not a shooting or terrorist attack." Ferny marched over and snapped on the top right button.

"No, no, the exact opposite." She beamed over at Avery. "You're one lucky miss, I'll say. One lucky miss." She faced the TV, knocking the screen. "It's not working."

"Hang on." Ferny drew her back as the old tube screen warmed up.

Avery stepped off the pedestal, anticipation firing as she waited for Prince Colin, who stood next to Madeline and Hyacinth in Old Towne Square, to speak.

He had no time to second-guess his move. Hero or a fool, he was committed. He woke with a solidifying resolve, got busy working on his Operation Humiliation, then donned his best suit, grabbed his rucksack carrying precious cargo, and joined the family Christmas breakfast, giving Avery a slow wink.

Her cheeks blushed with love. By the heat on his own face,

he suspected he did the same. But he kept his distance. Remained more friend than lover. If he did more than greet her, Colin feared he'd buckle and just propose right then and there.

But he wanted something grand. Over the top. Something worthy of Avery. And he wanted to put himself out there. To prove his sincerity.

His plan hit an initial snag when he realized Christmas Eve was on a Saturday. But a call to Madeline and Hyacinth's station bought him four minutes on the four o'clock news.

He requested Madeline and Hyacinth to host his appearance since they'd spent the entire Christmas season chasing the Pembroke bell tradition and Colin's love life. Since they were on scene yesterday when Avery was humiliated.

By four o'clock, the Christmas Eve sunset cast Old Towne Square in shadow. Avery would still get her sunset—

Madeline tapped his arm. "We're live in ten seconds. Are you ready?" She was dressed in a red coat with a green scarf.

Colin nodded. "I'm sorry to mess up your Christmas Eve. Thank you for coming."

"Please, love, we wouldn't miss this." She leaned close. "We're dying to know what you're going to do."

Dressed in green with a red scarf, Hyacinth came around to his left side. "Prince Colin, this is exciting . . ."

As they waited, the rucksack secure in his bare hand, last-minute shoppers stopped to stare. Photos were snapped. Behind them, the square's Christmas tree blinked with red, green, and white lights. In the distance, carolers harmonized, "*O come all ye faithful* . . ."

Madeline nudge him. "Live in three, two, one . . . Merry Christmas everyone. Madeline here along with my cohort, Hyacinth, in lovely Old Towne Square bringing you a special announcement from Prince Colin."

Despite the cold nip in the air, he was sweating.

"Merry Christmas, Prince Colin," Hyacinth said. "Do you have lots of presents round your tree?"

"My mum does. I don't even have a tree at my flat." The small talk wasn't helping.

"What? I put my tree up before Harvest Celebration."

"Perhaps next year."

"Prince Colin," Madeline said. "You called us with an important announcement this morning. Can you give us a clue what's on your mind?"

He inhaled, finding the words he'd practiced this morning before the mirror. "This business about the bell . . . I wanted to come clean with my story."

A light snow began to fall, the large flakes drifting through the golden gaslights.

"So you did ring the bell?"

"Not the first time. You see, I was in the tower, and I said a prayer." Why did speaking of his faith feel so awkward? Must be he needed to speak of it more.

"A prayer?" Madeline appeared confused.

"A prayer. About the woman I loved, and God rang the bell." Colin shifted his stance. He was about to propose publicly. Why not go all in for God as well? "I'm not fabricating, Maddie and Hy, but as my prayer left my lips, the bell began to ring. On its own. Guy Smoot will testify to that fact. If he has any integrity. It was a challenge for me to believe, I'll say."

"Really?" Hyacinth said, an air of unbelief in her tone. "Was it some sort of sign?"

Colin laughed. "I think so. I've been in love with Avery Truitt since the day I met her. My prayer was about her."

Hyacinth faced the camera. "For those of you who do *not* keep up with social media or the news at all, the prince met Princess Susanna's sister five years ago at the king's coronation."

"We went our separate ways for a while. But when I saw her at the Harvest Celebration, I knew my love for her had never died. Just hid away for a while."

"So what happened yesterday, Colin?" Madeline said. "When you left poor Miss Truitt alone in Old Towne Square?"

"One misfortune after another, including my phone being dropped from the ferry into the sea. But all that's behind us now." Slowly he lowered to one knee, his coat and part of his slacks sinking into the snow. He unzipped the rucksack, retrieving Granny's ring box. "Avery, I've blown it with you and have no right to expect you to trust me. At least not at the present time. Not with what I'm about to ask. But I'm going to ask you anyway." Madeline and Hyacinth's excited gasps billowed around him. "In the past, I was young and stupid and thought just ignoring how I truly felt would force us both to move on. But I realize I've never been too young or too immature when it came to loving you. The moment I met you, my world went right. I felt it. Like a click deep inside. Every man seeks to make his mark in the world, walk a path of greatness. Men rise and fall, fortunes are made and lost, but love, the rare beautiful jewel that is love, is the greatest legacy of all. I love you more than I can express in mere words." He raised the ring box to the camera and popped open the lid. Madeline and Hyacinth muted their squeals as they shifted and moved around behind him. "Avery Truitt, will you marry me? Please? Here's what I'm asking that requires all of your trust. Marry me Christmas morning at

Watchman Abbey. I'll be there at nine, on the steps, waiting for you. This is your chance to get even with me if you feel you must. You could leave me standing as I've left you in times past. Though I hope you won't. Please, if you have any compassion, any mercy, marry me."

The cameraman angled over Colin's hand, zooming in on the ring. And his four minutes was over.

CHAPTER 23

Avery teetered, trying to find a seat. In front of all Brighton, Prince Colin was on his knee, on live television, asking her to marry him.

"Lord a mercy." Mama slapped her hand over her heart. "Avery Mae, if you don't say yes, I'll say it for you. He already gave us two goats and a romantic public proposal. I can't ask for much more."

Susanna slipped her arm around her. "Welcome to the family, baby sister." Her watery voice said more than words.

"W-what do I do? I mean, do I call him? Oh, wait, he doesn't have a phone." Each pull of her breath, her trembling frame weakened.

"Look at her, shaking like a leaf. Melba, help her sit down." Ferny shoved a worn overstuffed chair forward. "Then call Handsome. Tell him I'm going to be working late."

"Ferny, no, I can't—"

Melba pressed Avery into the chair. She peered at Mama, then Susanna, hands clasped in her lap. "Do I say yes?"

"Of course." Susanna, so confident. "If that's what you want."

"I wish your daddy was here to see this." Mama's eyes glistened above her smile.

"I should go see Colin."

"No." Ferny, Melba, and Susanna, in unison.

"But what about all the arrangements? Won't we have to prepare?"

"Not we. He. Colin will be up half the night bribing florists, paying someone to decorate the abbey. He doesn't need much. A few bouquets of flowers. We've got food galore at the palace."

"We'll have a proper reception back at the Rib Shack when things settle down," Mama said.

"What about my dress?" She turned to the designer. "I can't ask you to give up your Christmas because we couldn't get our act together in time."

"You can and you will. Merry Christmas to me."

"Aves, this is about you and Colin. You can marry in blue jeans for all the outward matters. What's in your heart? Is he the man you want to marry?"

She wrapped her hands up with her sister's, her shaking easing, her confidence rising. "Maybe I didn't have a miracle like a ringing bell, but I know he is the one God has for me. Yes, I want to marry Colin. Yes!"

Susanna stood. "Ferny, what can we do to help? We're going to have a wedding in the morning."

At two a.m. Avery woke suddenly, a gentle tug on her heart. Slipping from her bed, she made her way to the window, shoved open the heavy sash, and leaned into the cold, greeting the young hours of this Christmas Day.

A hushed snow fell in large swirling flakes. The world was quiet. Peaceful, the amber lights of the city slipping over snow-covered rooftops.

"Merry Christmas, everyone," Avery whispered, then softly sang, *"All is calm, all is bright."*

In a little town some thousand of miles east of Stratton Palace, two thousand years ago, a King was born in a manger. The truest King of all. The One every nation will worship. He was, and is today, and will come again.

"Happy birthday, Jesus. Can't wait to meet You face-to-face. Say hi to Daddy for me."

Daddy. A fluttery ache drifted across her heart. "I wish you were here. I miss you so much."

She was about to go back to bed when a faint chime kept her at the window. Low and slow at first, from the direction of the Pembroke Chapel, the song grew louder and louder, until the palace grounds echoed with the glorious sound of the old tower's pealing bell.

CHAPTER 24

Christmas Day!

The morning dawned bright and beautiful, a fresh blanket of snow on the ground. All around the city, the cathedral bells rang out, heralding Christmas morn and the birth of the Lord.

Colin dressed in his white-and-blue naval uniform, his shoes shined to a mirror glaze. At eight thirty, he stepped out of his apartment toward the waiting carriage.

He'd spent every minute since his live proposal preparing for this morning, praying fervently Avery would accept him. He'd purchased a Christmas gift for her, diamond earrings, and had them wrapped under the small fake tree he bought for his apartment. It was a display model, completely decorated, on sale at Glidens. He hoped he'd be spending Christmas evening, and night, at home with his wife.

Mum offered her help, using her influence to find a florist. Colin ordered a bouquet of roses, mistletoe, ivy, and delicate fir branches. Mr. Franklin rang to say he would make a cake and deliver it to the palace.

Blessings flowed when a man said yes to his Father.

In a surprise show of support, Dad paid the groomsmen double time to polish up the gilded sleigh Mum inherited from her late father, King Leopold IV.

The two of them together offered to pay for a honeymoon. "Anywhere you like."

Colin graciously declined. "I'll fix it with Avery. I'd like to go wherever she wants. I think I've surprised her enough for one wedding."

Then Mum nudged Dad. "Go on, Eddie. No use stalling."

Dad cleared his throat. "I'm the one who alerted Madeline and Hyacinth."

Colin regarded him for a long, hot moment. "I knew you were against us but—"

"I must apologize." Dad glanced at Mum. "I was wrong. In the spirit of the season, I ask your forgiveness."

"Of course, Dad," Colin said. "Do you understand this was my decision before God? For Avery and me? Can you accept us?"

Dad raised his chin, absorbing the pushback from his son. "I can. I want you to know I'm proud of you, Colin. I will support your decision and welcome Avery into our family."

His reply caught in Colin's emotion. He was tired from a restless night and a long day of preparations. "Th-thank you, Dad." Their hug was sincere, sealed with the back slap of approval.

The archbishop agreed to officiate after the early Christmas service. The abbey organist would play. The grounds yeoman set out barriers along Abbey Road, the short narrow lane running in front of the church, and rolled out the red carpet since it was tradition for the brides of princes to walk down the road on red carpet.

Everything was done. Except for Avery's answer. Colin stood at the main sanctuary doors, his gaze fixed down the road.

He deserved to be stood up. But by the mercy of God, Avery would appear around the bend in the road at any moment.

The quiet from the early morning dissipated with the throngs filling the street. Hundreds of policemen and constables lined Stratton Boulevard, keeping the crowds at bay.

When Avery exited the palace in her flowing white Ferny gown, the roar from the street pressed her back. Subtle shouts broke through.

"Happy Christmas!"

"Happy wedding day!"

She slid into the car with Nathaniel, Susanna, and Mama. As the driver made his way out of the palace, Avery stared out the window.

"They all came out on Christmas morning?"

Nathaniel's laugh was loving, almost fatherly. "You were proposed to publicly by a prince. They had to see if you were going to meet him at the abbey."

Avery laughed. "Now they all know before he does."

"Serves him right," Susanna said. She looked beautiful in a red gown with white trim. Mama wore the gown she planned to wear to the ball, the pale green bringing out her eyes.

The entire ride to the abbey, curious and well-wishers lined the street. Vendors even, dotting the curbs, selling cups of coffee and hot cocoa. Franklin's Bakery held up bags of freshly baked puffs.

When the king's car slid past, the people stopped whatever they were doing and cheered, waving.

"We can't go any farther," the driver said, glancing back at Avery. "Too many people. But we're right at the tip of Abbey Road. Miss Avery, are you doing the traditional walk?"

She glanced at Susanna. "Am I?"

"Absolutely."

She climbed out, Susanna and Mama helping with her gown, protection officers surrounding.

"Avery." Nathaniel bent close. "Are you sure you don't want me or your mama to walk down the aisle? I'd be happy to escort you."

"Thank you." Her eyes misted as she peered up at him. "But I want to walk this alone." She squeezed his arm, her eyes welling up. "Besides, I'm not really alone. Daddy's in my heart and God is with me. Always."

The king kissed her cheek. "As are we. Go on now, Colin is probably outside his mind wondering if you're coming."

Avery started forward, her heart overflowing. The crowd pressed in close, their faces so real and joyful. "Merry Christmas," she said. "Thank you all for coming."

Security forbade her from stopping to shake hands, so she made her way, waving, more and more undone by the generosity of the Brightonians. They should be at home with their families.

She caught her breath when the red runner appeared, then she made her way toward the curve in the cobblestone avenue, the leaning crowd obscuring her view of the abbey.

She glanced at the protection officers. "Let me go on alone. I'll be fine."

A few more steps and she spied her groom, Prince Colin,

handsome and regal in his navy uniform, scanning the lane for a glimpse of her.

Was she coming? It was after nine now. The cathedral clocks had chimed the hour, though to Colin it seemed an eternity had ticked past. From the crowd, someone started a carol. "*I heard the bells on Christmas day . . .*"

Colin joined in, singing softly, more to calm his raging heartbeat than anything else. Would the Christmas wedding bells ring for him?

"*. . . the old familiar carols played.*"

Mid-chorus, the song stopped with a collective, deep gasp from the people. A boisterous roar followed.

She was coming.

Pulse pounding, Colin skipped down the steps, moving toward the road, angling to see round the people. As he passed, the crowd parted, and there she came, hurrying toward him, her skirt swishing over the red carpet, a feathery wrap about her pale shoulders, the family and protection officers striding after her.

Colin froze mid-motion. She was stunning, stealing every piece of his heart. *Avery, love . . .* A swell of pride flooded his chest. *Lord, please let me always be worthy of her.*

He wanted to call her name but emotion tripped his words. So he shoved forward, down the runner to meet her.

"Colin!" She launched into his arms, her face tucked against the curve of his neck.

"You came." He twirled her about, his heart playing a symphony in his chest. When he set her down, the crowd cheered.

She tapped her forehead to his. "Wouldn't miss it."

"Want to get married?"

"Yes, I do."

Gripping her hand in his, he led her toward the abbey, his smile so broad his cheeks ached. The crowd cheered and wished them well.

Inside the nave, Colin reached round the carved, polished table for her bouquet.

"I hope this will do."

"Colin, it's beautiful."

He looped her arm through his and walked into the sanctuary where Dad waited with Mum and his sisters.

"Welcome to the Tattersalls," Dad said, taking hold of Avery's shoulders, kissing her forehead.

"Thank you, sir." She offered her hand. "I hope we can be friends."

Dad's eyes glistened as he shook her hand. "I'm sure we can."

"I love your son very much."

"I suspect he loves you even more."

Colin bent his lips to her ear. "Want to be really different, love?"

She faced him, glistening eye to glistening eye. "Why be normal?"

He tipped his head toward the door. "Let's marry outside, on the red runner. We've thousands of guests. Let's not leave them out in the cold on Christmas morn."

"Let's do it. For all those who took time on Christmas to see if this moment would ever arrive."

The archbishop huffed and puffed, citing it was highly unusual for a prince to marry in the street, but what about this wedding was normal? So, wrapped in his priestly robes, he led the way out of the abbey and down to the street.

Beside and behind them, the protection detail scurried to make way.

"You will all be our witnesses," Colin said.

The citizens responded with wild delight.

From the abbey tower, the cathedral bells rang out, calling across the city, filling the air with cheer. *The prince is getting married.*

When they arrived at the end of the lane, the archbishop stopped, fumbling with his wedding book.

"Prince Colin, please face your bride."

Dad and Mum, his sisters, Nathaniel and Susanna, Glo Truitt and Queen Campbell, Henry, and Prince Stephen and Princess Corina gathered round.

And half of Cathedral City. At least it felt that way. Colin was quite sure he caught a glimpse of Madeline and Hyacinth and their cameraman.

The cathedral bells died down as Colin intertwined his fingers with Avery's. The breeze drifting between them hushed and the winter sun peeked through the clouds.

"Dearly beloved . . ."

As the archbishop began the wedding sermon, a faint clang echoed in the distance. Colin glanced round, squeezing Avery's hand. Did she hear . . .

There it was again. A clear, distinct chime coming from Pembroke Chapel way.

"It's the bell," Avery whispered. "God is ringing it for us."

"I believe He is, darling." Colin couldn't hold in his laugh. "I believe He is."

EPILOGUE

As the story goes . . .

It's said that the chapel bell never rang properly after the marriage of Prince Colin and Avery Truitt. Not even when the king sent men out to repair it.

But year after year, between Harvest and Christmas, some in the nearby boroughs claimed to hear the clang of the bell. Just once. But a clang nonetheless.

Forgotten was the deathly legend of Prince Michael. A new one of love prevailed.

Upon his marriage, King Nathaniel II styled his cousin, Prince Colin, His Royal Highness, and his wife, Princess Avery of Brighton.

She became a volleyball coach, and for the rest of her days championed education and girls' athletics across the kingdom.

Prince Colin inherited his father's dynasty and became one of the wealthiest and most generous men in Europe.

They raised two princes and two princesses, numerous dogs,

cats, rabbits, and untold number of goats. Fred and Ethel were quite procreant. To this day, their grandchildren keep the Tattersall mews filled with the sound of bleating.

King Nathaniel and Princess Susanna had five children. The oldest, Princess Honor, became queen upon her sixtieth birthday, Nathaniel having lived to a ripe old age.

Prince Stephen and Princess Corina raised three princes and left a legacy of loving well throughout Brighton and the world.

Mama Truitt, Glo, sold the Rib Shack to Uncle Hud not long after Avery married and left St. Simons, taking up residence in Cathedral City. She became Granny not only to her children's children but to the children of Brighton. She and Queen Campbell were the best of friends until their old bones went to rest.

But when lore is told around Brighton Kingdom these days, and romantic notions of happily ever after are spoken of in dreamy voices, it's Prince Colin and Princess Avery the young lads and lasses think upon.

For in all their days, for all their wealth and achievements, the greatest thing ever said of them was, "No one loved like they loved."

Prince Colin once said, "My greatest treasures are my wife and children. I'm aware that when I stand before the Lord of all the ages and He judges my life, He will ask first and foremost if I learned to love my wife and children more than myself. I hope when I say yes, He replies, 'Well done.'"

So you see, Prince Colin and Princess Avery, and all the Strattons, Truitts, and Tattersalls, indeed lived happily ever after.

And isn't that what fairy tales are all about?

DISCUSSION QUESTIONS

1. Avery and Prince Colin fell in love at a young age. Many of us—or our parents—married young. Today we want "kids" to wait. What do you think of our hero and heroine falling in love? Did you fall in love in high school or college?

2. Prince Colin's father was against his son marrying young, as well as marrying an American. Was he right to interfere? What role do parents have in their adult children's lives? Especially if they are still in school or dependent on support.

3. Post college, Avery is trying to find her footing. Talk about how you managed finding a career or job after high school or college. Did you see God working in your life?

4. Prince Colin rather abruptly ended his relationship with Avery. He thought it was for the best. What do you think? Has something similar happened to you? Did you ever

feel the need to just cut someone off? Talk about the ramifications.

5. Christmas in Brighton Kingdom sounds magical! What are some of your favorite memories of Christmas.

6. Would you want to be married on Christmas day?

7. Traditions play a role in this story. Talk about your family or personal holiday traditions. What about in your community?

8. When Avery was decorating the Christmas tree at the Rib Shack, she realized she couldn't have Christmas without the Cross. Have you seen that revelation in your life?

9. What did you think of the snowy cupcake fight?

10. Prince Colin and Avery have a lot of communication mishaps. How can we overcome those moments in our lives, especially during the holidays?

11. Avery had to learn to trust Colin. But he had to learn to listen to God above men. Even his father. How important is it to make this transition in our lives?

12. How can you show love to someone during this Christmas season?

13. How have you seen God "ring the bell" in answer to your prayers? Encourage one another with answered prayer stories.

ACKNOWLEDGMENTS

From the moment Avery and Prince Colin met in *Once Upon a Prince*, I knew their story had to be told. And from the amount of reader requests, you did too. Thank you!

Special shout out to:

My editor Becky Philpott, who also believed in the young prince and Georgia girl. I'm grateful.

My publisher, Daisy Hutton, and the fiction team at HarperCollins Christian Publishing for your support.

Karli Jackson, for your hard work on this book and help bringing it to life.

Susan May Warren for being there with hammer and chisel to find the story in the "block of an idea." Love you friend.

Beth K. Vogt for sounding out story points and helping with volleyball terminology. Any and all mistakes are mine. Much love!

My husband, a good man, a gift from God to me. He knows

how to kick me back into play when I say, "This story is just not working."

All the fans of the Royal Wedding Series, I so appreciate you!

Jesus, the Son of God, the Son of Man, who is the reason we love and celebrate Christmas. I love you.

ABOUT THE AUTHOR

Rachel Hauck is the *New York Times, Wall Street Journal,* and *USA Today* bestselling author of *The Wedding Dress,* which was also named Inspirational Novel of the Year by *Romantic Times* and was a RITA finalist. Rachel lives in central Florida with her husband and two pets and writes from her ivory tower.

Visit her online at rachelhauck.com
Facebook: @rachelhauck
Twitter: @RachelHauck
Instagram: @rachelhauck

The Royal Wedding Series

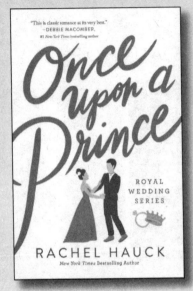

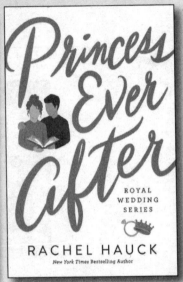

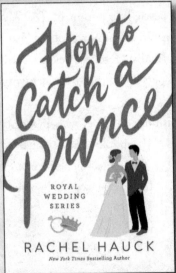

AVAILABLE IN PRINT, E-BOOK, AND AUDIO